GE

The general flicked his hand, and four of his soldiers dashed forward. It wasn't until they reached Fargo that he realized they were closing in like four hungry wolves for the kill.

In a flash Fargo drew his Colt and fired. He winged the first soldier, who fell back screaming. As the second closed in, Fargo swung the Colt, catching the man across the face. The Mexican went down to his knees, then fell forward. Fargo spun about and lashed out with a kick that caught the third man full in the belly, crunching his ribs. The fourth one jumped him from behind, and Fargo felt the man's powerful arms locked around him. Fargo relaxed, as if giving up, then suddenly tossed the man in a somersault over his head. The Trailsman leapt on him, but it was unnecessary. The man was out cold.

Fargo pointed his gun toward the general's chest. But he found himself facing the barrels of two dozen rifles.

All Fargo could do was shout, "What the hell's going on?"

He had a sinking feeling he was about to find out. . . .

BE SURE TO READ THE OTHER BOOKS IN THE EXCITING TRAILSMAN SERIES!

PROMISED LAND

Jason Manning

Legendary mountain man Hugh Falconer was not free to choose where to go as he led a wagon train he had saved from slaughter at the hands of a white renegade, a half-breed killer, and a marauding Pawnee war party. Falconer took the people he was sworn to protect, and a woman he could not help wanting, into a secluded valley to survive until spring.

But there was one flaw in his plan that turned this safe haven into a terror trap. A man was there before them ... a man who ruled the valley as his private kingdom ... a mountain man whose prowess matched Falconer's own ... a man with whom Falconer had to strike a devil's bargain to avoid a bloodbath ... or else fight no-holds-barred to the death ... or both....

from **SIGNET**

THE

TRAILSMAN

#175

BETRAYAL AT
EL DIABLO

by

Jon Sharpe

A SIGNET BOOK

SIGNET
Published by the Penguin Group
Penguin Books USA Inc., 375 Hudson Street,
New York, New York 10014, U.S.A.
Penguin Books Ltd, 27 Wrights Lane,
London W8 5TZ, England
Penguin Books Australia Ltd, Ringwood,
Victoria, Australia
Penguin Books Canada Ltd, 10 Alcorn Avenue,
Toronto, Ontario, Canada M4V 3B2
Penguin Books (N.Z.) Ltd, 182-190 Wairau Road,
Auckland 10, New Zealand

Penguin Books Ltd, Registered Offices:
Harmondsworth, Middlesex, England

First published by Signet, an imprint of Dutton Signet,
a division of Penguin Books USA Inc.

First Printing, July, 1996
10 9 8 7 6 5 4 3 2 1

The first chapter of this book originally appeared in *Death Valley Bloodbath*, the one hundred seventy-fourth volume in this series.

🄿 REGISTERED TRADEMARK—MARCA REGISTRADA

Printed in the United States of America

The Trailsman

Beginnings . . . they bend the tree and they mark the man. Skye Fargo was born when he was eighteen. Terror was his midwife, vengeance his first cry. Killing spawned Skye Fargo, ruthless, cold-blooded murder. Out of the acrid smoke of gunpowder still hanging in the air, he rose, cried out a promise never forgotten.

The Trailsman they began to call him all across the West: searcher, scout, hunter, the man who could see where others only looked, his skills for hire but not his soul; the man who lived each day to the fullest, yet trailed each tomorrow. Skye Fargo, the Trailsman, and the seeker who could take the wildness of a land and the wanting of a woman and make them his own.

El Diablo, Mexico, 1860—
a vast labyrinth of canyons and blistering heat,
bandidos, thirst, and stalking death,
where legends said the killing land
could burn a man's body and soul to ash . . .

1

"Senor Fargo, please. I am told you can help me," the padre said, running his hand nervously over his bald pate. The ruddy light of the rising sun lit the wide, dry valley, the dark forms of the cattle herd down below, and accentuated the deep lines of the old padre's face. Life in old Mexico, even for men of the Church, was damned hard.

"You must be Father Salvatore. I heard you've been looking for me," Fargo said, throwing the saddle across the glistening Ovaro. He patted the trusty pinto's neck and it whinnied, eager to hit the trail. "What's up?" He bent to the task of cinching.

"The town of Los Ricos—" the padre began nervously, then stopped. Fargo shot a look across the saddle to tell the old man he was listening, and the padre continued. "I was passing through. There was a man named Gregorio, the owner of the local cantina. As soon as he saw me arrive, he told me to get out, that the whole town was doomed. That everyone would die."

"The whole town, huh?" Fargo asked. He checked his canteens. Yeah, both full. And pemmi-

9

can in the saddlebags. Bullets. Blanket. Matches. "And you believed him?"

"He was not crazy," Father Salvatore said, coming around the horse to stand beside him. "I am sure. But he was scared and kept looking over his shoulder. The next day we were going to meet at the cantina and he promised to tell me everything he suspected. Why he was afraid. But the next day he was gone. And he never came back." Father Salvatore glanced up at Fargo. "I know what you are thinking," he continued. "But I cannot explain. I saw something wrong in the town. The people, they were afraid. Something terrible will happen there but I do not know what. Everybody knows the reputation of the Trailsman, the man who can find the tracks others do not see. There is some invisible evil in this town."

"Los Ricos," Fargo said thoughtfully. "I've heard of the place. Never been to the town, but I know the El Diablo." Yeah, he knew the man-killing desert land and it was about the last place on earth he wanted to ride through. There were a helluva lot nicer trails heading north. Fargo gazed across the sere hills of the ranch land at the herd of longhorns he'd spent the last two weeks getting back from some two-bit Mexican bandidos with the help of his Apache friend, Akando. The job was done now and his pocket was full of cash from the grateful Mexican ranchers. He'd planned to head up to Fort Worth for a wild couple of weeks at Hell's Half Acre. Women, booze, cards, and catching up with some old friends. Fargo shot a look at Akando, who stood nearby beside his Appaloosa.

He and Akando had ridden many trails together before, and the Apache was a loyal friend. The Indian was a damn fine tracker and hunter, silent as the wind, wise as an eagle, fierce as a cougar. There were few men Fargo liked better as a trail companion. They seemed to always understand each other without the need for words. Now Akando's face was as unreadable and stony as a cliff, but his black eyes flicked toward the old monk and glittered with curiosity at the padre's words.

Father Salvatore saw Fargo's hesitation and opened the leather pouch that hung from his rope belt. "Senor Fargo, I beg you. I know in my heart there is trouble there in Los Ricos. I will give you money, pay your fee."

"Keep your pesos for the poor," Fargo answered. He patted the old man's shoulder. "Akando and I will head north through El Diablo. We'll stop in at Los Ricos and have a talk with this—"

"Gregorio," the padre said hastily. "His name is Gregorio, at the cantina."

"Yeah," Fargo said. He swung into the saddle and Akando did the same.

"They were right," Padre Salvatore said excitedly, as if disbelieving his own words. "Yes, they were right. They said go to Senor Fargo because he is a good man." The padre pulled the long rosary from where it hung on his rope belt and held the large wooden cross in the air. With a nod to the old monk, Fargo touched his heel to the Ovaro's flank and he was off, heading across the dry mesquite plain, followed by Akando. "I will pray for you, Senor Fargo," the padre called after them. "Every day, I will pray to the Virgin Mary to keep you safe. And St. Christopher, too. Every day I will . . ."

The old man's voice was lost in the distance and the sound of the horses' hoofbeats on the trail. Fargo shook his head, thinking of Forth Worth and one particular dove he remembered there. Oh, hell. Maybe this Los Ricos thing would turn out to be a mistake and they could ride on. On the other hand, if there was trouble brewing up ahead at Los Ricos, Fargo thought, it was bound to find him anyway. He never needed to go looking for it.

He and Akando rode for a half hour across the ranch land, then turned their horses northward into the hills and toward the desert hell known as El Diablo.

The hawk was floating in a wide circle high in the white-hot sky, half a mile off the trail to the west. There was only one thing that made a hawk spin in the sky like that. Something dead below. Hidden in a mesquite-choked gully. And it was a fresh kill, too.

Fargo reined in the black-and-white pinto beside the tower of red rocks. The sweat-foamed Ovaro came to a halt and shifted under him, shaking its mane. The midday sun blazed down, the heat ris-

12

ing in waves from the rocks and dry sand. Fargo's eyes narrowed as he squinted up at the blasting sun and at the slowly circling hawk. His hand instinctively moved to the butt of the Henry rifle in the saddle scabbard. Trouble? His instinct said yes. Honed to the sharpness of a fresh-stropped blade by years of living in the wilds of the West, his sixth sense told him something was wrong in the vast landscape around him. He doffed his hat, mopped the sweat off his face, and glanced back at Akando.

The Apache had spotted the hawk, too, and had come to a halt on his Appaloosa. His hand rested on the hilt of the knife stuck in the buckskin sheath at his waist. His carmine face and muscular chest were glossy with sweat, and beneath the red band around his black shining hair, his keen eyes were silent with a question.

Skye Fargo nodded at Akando, then glanced out at the horizon. In the distance, across a baked salt flat, a cloud of dust hid the party of riders they'd been following for three days. Not on purpose. Three days before, just as they'd entered El Diablo, they picked up the trail of five riders going the same direction ahead of them. The first night, while Akando guarded their horses, Fargo had crept up on the strangers' camp to spy them out. There were four men and a woman—a young and beautiful woman with waist-length black hair and a voluptuous figure, Fargo had noted. A tall gentleman, dapper and imperious, with a silver-chased hat on his silver hair, seemed to be the leader of the group. The riders' clothing struck Fargo as vaguely foreign. More than that, he couldn't learn. So he and Akando had followed along behind, staying far enough in the rear that the riders had no idea they were there.

Not many ventured into El Diablo. It was killing land. Anybody riding across it had to be desperate for something. Fargo had wondered many times during the past three days what brought the party of five foreigners to El Diablo. But he had enough on his mind right now to want to get into somebody else's business. If there was one thing you learned in El Diablo country, it was to keep your distance.

Now Fargo's lake-blue eyes followed the sudden flapping of a vulture above the mesquite that choked the dry riverbed to the west. What was the fresh kill out there? Likely a peccary, the bristly wild boar. Or else a cougar had flipped an armadillo and gorged on its soft underbelly. Probably nothing more than that. The riders they were following had swept right by without noticing. But his instinct told him to take a look. There were three hawks up in the sky now. Without a word, Fargo turned the Ovaro off the trail and Akando followed.

They wound through the thick mesquite and paloverde until they spotted the dusty black flapping of vultures ahead. Fargo dismounted and walked over for a closer look. The story was as clear as words on paper to one who could read the signs. Fargo clapped his hands loudly and waved his arms. The half-dozen vultures hopped away reluctantly, then flew to perches on nearby trees where they hunched their ugly pink necks and kept close watch.

The two Mexicans lay sprawled faceup in the blistering sun, their faces already disfigured by the vultures. They'd been dead about two hours. Dark bloody chests. Both shot dead center, close range. Powder burns—real close range. Their mouths gaped open, black blood staining what was left of their skin. Their tongues had been cut out.

"Gomez," Akando said as he spotted the dark, gaping, empty mouths. Even in the one word the Apache uttered, Fargo heard a note of wonder.

The Gomez gang. Fargo hadn't heard about them for ten years. Jorge Gomez and his bandidos had rampaged through Mexico, robbing and pillaging. Mostly stagecoaches and shipments from Mexico City. Whenever anyone crossed them, the brutal gang cut out his tongue. Then Gomez and his band just seemed to disappear into El Diablo. Now, here they were again.

The Apache turned and began circling the spot, reading the tracks in the dust. Fargo remained looking down at the bodies. They might be father and son. Their rough woven serapes, battered sombreros, and calloused hands marked them as poor men. Probably locals. The younger one wore a stained leather vest tooled with pictures of running horses and a pair of cheap spurs attached to his woven sandals, as if he had aspirations to become a wandering *vaquero*, hired by the rich gringos up north. But who were they?

Fargo knelt and quickly went through their pockets but found no clues. A silver glint at the neck of the older one caught Fargo's attention. He leaned over and yanked the chain from around the man's neck. A cloud of black flies swarmed, sounding angry in the heat. Dangling from the glittering chain was a piece of carved turquoise in the shape of a turtle. He'd show it around at Los Ricos. Maybe somebody would recognize it and know who the men were.

As Fargo moved away from the bodies, the vultures flew down. In the dust all around, the tracks were confusing. Cattle. Horses. Even a mule. Akando stepped out of the mesquite and wordlessly motioned him to come look. There, hidden in the brush, were the marks where horses had been tethered and where men had slept the night without a fire. Suddenly Akando squatted down and peered at the ground. Fargo leaned over him.

"They came from hills," Akando said, pointing west to the low, bare mounds, "and went back that way, too." And they'd driven off the cattle that the two Mexicans had been herding. The Gomez gang—or whoever had killed the men—was many miles away by now.

They rose and scoured the area again, but could find nothing else of use. As they mounted, Fargo thought of the five riders up ahead. The dust cloud was barely visible on the horizon now, since the riders had got far ahead of them while they stopped to search the gully.

"Let's pull in closer," Fargo said as they set off through the brush. Akando touched his moccasined heels to the sides of his Appaloosa and the horse sprang into a gallop. The Ovaro bounded forward. Fargo felt a sudden concern for the foreigners, especially for the woman. If Jorge Gomez and his bandidos were still lurking around, there was bound to be another ambush. Of course, the Gomez gang was now driving the few stolen cattle and horses—something puzzled Fargo about that. Gomez had been famous for intercepting gold shipments, lifting jewels off wealthy lady travelers, and carrying away safes of cash from the rich ranchers. A few head of cattle from two poor Mexicans didn't seem like Gomez's style. Still, their tongues had been cut out. Now who else would have done that?

The Ovaro and Appaloosa kept easy pace as they galloped down the hard-packed and curving streambed until they came to a rocky area. Fargo led them up through the brush and out of the wash. At the edge of the cracked salt flat, Fargo paused for a moment.

Before them, the white cracked land glittered in the broiling sun. On the far side, the dust cloud that hid the five riders before was now completely gone, dissipated among the jagged teeth of red rock that rimmed the flat. And that worried him. If he and Akando galloped straight across the glaring expanse, it would make them completely visible to anyone within fifteen miles and they would come up to the towering red rocks utterly exposed. He and Akando could outride or outshoot anybody. But there was no telling what lay ahead. Fargo's eyes traced a path along the eastern edge of the flat, along a string of low red mesas. Riding at the foot of them would make their dust plume less visible, he decided. He nodded toward the east.

"Good," Akando agreed as he loosened the rifle in his saddle. They rode fast now, the horses pulling hard, in a lather, making a wide arc along the broken mesas. A few miles later, they approached the edge of the flat and slowed to a walk as they rode in among the tall red rocks. Fargo didn't like the feel of the area—too many places somebody could be hiding. He glanced back at Akando and saw his eyes alert, his body tensed, listening. It was impossible to see far ahead. Fargo spotted the tracks of the five riders and they began to follow, winding up a gentle grade.

They had not gone far when the pop of gunfire broke out ahead of them and a woman screamed. They galloped forward as the sound of gunfire grew nearer. Fargo's Colt was in his hand, its silver barrel flashing in the sun. He heard men shouting and the gunfire redoubled.

Suddenly, the rocks ended and Fargo saw in the clearing ahead the rising smoke of battle. He reined in and instantly his eyes took in every-thing—the five riders pinned down in a circle of rocks, their horses scattered in terror as the lead flew through the air. There were ambushers hiding in the rocks around the clearing. He watched the rising gunsmoke. Two. No, three. He dismounted and with one look told Akando they'd split up. Running fast and low, keeping the rocks between himself and the ambushers, he dashed from cover to cover, making his way up the slope until he spotted one of the men and came up behind him. He was a scrawny-looking fellow in a serape, hunched down behind a rock, popping up from time to time to take a shot at the travelers down below.

Fargo moved forward slowly, his Colt in hand, until he was a few yards behind the man.

"Freeze," Fargo said. "I gotcha covered."

The ambusher jumped, then whirled about, dropping his gun. Fargo felt a wave of surprise course through him. It was a kid. Probably twelve years old. And terrified, his dark eyes wide and his mouth hanging open. He slowly raised his hands.

"Move forward," Fargo said. "Slow. Away from the gun." He motioned with the barrel of the Colt in case the kid didn't speak English. The kid took a few steps forward.

Suddenly, a bullet whined by Fargo, grazing his cheek and shattering the rock behind him. There was another fusillade of gunfire from below and one of the bullets caught the kid in the back. He pitched forward, a look of surprise on his face.

"Hold your fire!" Fargo yelled, hitting the dirt as more bullets whistled by. "Hold your fire!" He crawled forward to where the kid lay and rolled him over, but his dark eyes were blank. He'd died instantly. Fargo swore. What the hell was a kid doing out here?

There was a sudden scramble in the rocks above, and Fargo saw a second ambusher, another small, skinny kid dressed in peasant clothes, high-tailing it up the slope. He was probably heading for his horse. Fargo ran after him through the rocks until he caught sight of the boy, who was un-tethering his mount.

"Halt," Fargo called out, cocking his pistol. The figure turned and Fargo saw another young Mexican boy. Scared, too. The kid raised his rifle but it was shaking in his hand.

"Drop it," Fargo commanded. The kid paused a moment, then threw down his gun. Suddenly, he jerked at the bridle of his horse and started to swing onto it. Fargo leaped forward, grabbed the bridle, pulled the kid down from the horse, then hauled him up by his shirt collar. On the far side of the ravine, he heard the gunfire continue and guessed that Akando was over there.

"Who the hell are you?" Fargo said, shaking him. The boy was no more than twelve and his frightened eyes were ringed with dark circles. One thing was for sure. The kid hadn't come on his own. "Who sent you here?"

The kid swore in Spanish and Fargo shook him again.

"Answer me. Who sent you here?"

"Ramirez," the kid panted, holding his bleeding shoulder. "The generalissimo." He looked up at Fargo as if that explained everything. Fargo had heard of General Vito Ramirez, famous in all of Mexico as an Indian fighter and a powerful politician.

"You're not part of the army," Fargo said disbelievingly.

"No. Ramirez." The boy spat in the dust at the name. "We find him. Me and my brothers. Over there." The boy jerked his head in the direction of the travelers. Fargo had seen pictures of the generalissimo and he knew the kid was mistaken. The famous Ramirez was not with the five riders.

"You were trying to *ambush* Generalissimo Ramirez?" Fargo said. The boy nodded his head vigorously.

The gunfire had ceased and there were voices calling from down below. Fargo heard footsteps and turned to see the tall gentleman he'd spotted before heading toward him, running from cover to cover, a pearl-handled revolver in his hand. He was followed by another man, the biggest of the bunch.

"It's all right," Fargo called out. "I'm a friend. And I got your enemy here."

The gentleman stepped forward warily. Sunlight

sparkled on his silver-chased hat and silver hair, which was worn long. His boots were of the best tooled leather. His face, narrow and long, had a strong jaw and prominent cheekbones. Under his heavy lids, the dark brown eyes looked at everything coolly, as if he were weary, bored. One of the other men, a big fellow in black, followed with a rifle.

"Who are you?" the gentleman asked in Spanish, his revolver covering both of them.

"I just saved your necks," Fargo snapped back. The tall gentleman smiled very slowly, his black brows arched imperiously.

"So you did," he said slowly, lowering his gun. "I am Prospero Aznar, Count of Seville." He drew himself up importantly and glared at Fargo. So, he'd been right, Fargo thought. The riders were foreigners, all the way from Spain.

"And this is my man, Manrique." The count waved in the direction of the big man who stepped out from behind a rock. The big man's face was as pitted as the moon and his eyes were sunk deep in his face. "And who is this—this peasant?" The count looked disdainfully at the boy.

"He thinks you're Generalissimo Vito Ramirez," Fargo said.

Prospero Aznar seemed stunned for a moment, then laughed heartily. So did the big fellow, Manrique. The kid squirmed in Fargo's grip and glanced from one to the other, his eyes dark and miserable.

"Why were you looking for Ramirez?" Fargo asked the kid again.

"Because of . . . because Gomez," the kid said. "Los Ricos. The generalissimo, he is making us—"

The shot took Fargo by surprise, the bullet exploding from Manrique's pistol, catching the kid in the belly. A look of pain passed over the young kid's face in an instant and then he slumped to the ground. A trickle of blood darkened the gritty sand. The puff of gunsmoke blew away in the breeze.

"What the hell?" Fargo swore. He took a menacing step toward the big man. "What the hell did you do that for?"

"He was a stupid kid," Manrique said, holstering his gun. "A nobody. He was nothing."

"A peasant," Aznar agreed. He pulled a silk handkerchief from his pocket and mopped his face. "It is a waste of time to listen to peasant talk."

Fargo felt the rage rise in him and he barreled forward, lashed out, driving a fist into Manrique's smooth jaw. The big man stumbled backward for an instant, and then his pocked face darkened. Manrique sprang forward and grabbed Fargo by the neck. They went down and rolled in the dust, over and over, struggling for a grip. The big fellow was strong, his arms like iron.

Fargo rolled on top of him and landed a right square in Manrique's belly, then a left uppercut that threw his head back against the hard ground.

But Manrique rallied, swore in Spanish, and suddenly began pummeling with his fists, a pounding flurry that caught Fargo in the belly, the jaw, the chest. The big man's fists were huge, like meaty clubs, and he knew how to use them, too. The two of them pulled apart and got wearily to their feet, facing off.

Manrique's eyes were emotionless, empty, intent on his prey. Fargo became aware of others approaching as the big man closed in. He didn't like the idea of duking it out with the rest of Aznar's company surrounding him. It was time to get this over with. Summoning all his strength, Fargo drew back his powerful arm and delivered a forceful blow that caught Manrique square on the jaw, almost snapping his head around. The big man staggered backward with the force of the impact, blinking his eyes. His knees weakened and he suddenly went down, his eyes rolling back in his head.

Fargo mopped the sweat off his face with his sleeve and looked around at the others, who had come up from down below.

"Oh, Father! Are you all right?"

The young woman was running toward the count. She was even more exquisite up close. She was short, her figure extravagantly rounded, with a tiny waist and high mounded breasts that poured over the top of her low-cut black dress. Her waist-length hair gleamed like black fire in the sunlight. She glanced at Fargo and he felt immediately that there was something catlike in her face, with its

24

quiet dark eyes that seemed to see everything, wide cheekbones, and pointed chin. She noticed his gaze and glanced back at him, smiling, transformed in an instant into a kittenish young woman.

Following her like a panting bloodhound was a pale redheaded fellow in plaid pants and shirt. In his hand, he carried a forked stick. Serena reached her father and wrapped her arms around him as he patted her on the shoulder.

"I am fine, Serena. We are safe now." The count glanced over at Fargo, as if he wanted to apologize. "Senor . . ."

"Fargo. Skye Fargo."

"Ah, Senor Fargo. My apologies for the behavior of my man, Manrique. He can be so hotheaded." The count offered his hand. Fargo felt Serena watching him closely, her eyes traveling unabashedly over his hard muscled body, his powerful chest.

Fargo nodded but refused to shake with the count, still burned up by Aznar's words. Still angry that Manrique had shot the kid before he'd had a chance to find out what this was all about. It was as if Manrique wanted to hush up the kid before he could talk. The count and his daughter huddled some distance away with the other man, a smaller version of Manrique, who had followed Serena up the slope.

Meanwhile, the redheaded fellow poked curiously at the dead peasant boy with one end of his stick. Fargo went over to the body and stared down at it. Damn shame. Two dead kids and no answers. Akando had undoubtedly gone after the third kid. Fargo glanced around but saw no sign of the Apache.

"The kid was looking for Generalissimo Ramirez," Fargo muttered, almost to himself. The redhead looked up at the words.

"Ramirez!" he exclaimed. "Why, ain't that a coincidence? We was just waiting for the generalissimo to show up here." Fargo's thoughts whirled but he kept his face poker still. So, the kid hadn't been far wrong. "By the by, I'm Hagan Crowley. Seeker and finder." Crowley pulled on his plaid jacket and stuck out one hand.

"Seeker and finder of what?" Fargo asked Crowley. Hagan Crowley raised his forked stick with the other hand.

"Water in the desert," Hagan Crowley said grandly, waving his stick in the air. "I can find silver in the streams. Husbands who have run away. Kidnapped children. Lost horses. Missing cattle. Buried treasure—"

"That's enough," the count snapped, overhearing Hagan Crowley's words. He turned to Fargo and said in a different tone of voice, "Tell me, Senor Skye Fargo, what brings you to El Diablo?"

"You're Skye Fargo?" Crowley asked, turning to him in amazement. "The one they call the Trailsman?"

26

Fargo scratched his neck and didn't bother to answer.

"Hot damn," Crowley said excitedly. "Well, this is my lucky day. I always wanted to meet you, Fargo. Been hearing tell of you for years." He poked his elbow at the count. "This Trailsman fellow is real smart, real brave. Real famous, too."

"Really," said Count Aznar coolly. Fargo had the feeling the count was less than pleased. But Serena was looking at him with a smile.

"So, just what brings you to this country?" the count asked.

"Just passing through," Fargo replied. Yeah, he'd keep his business to himself for now. "Where are you heading?"

"A little peasant village you've never heard of," the count said, smiling.

"It's a town called Los Ricos," Serena said, and her eyes glittered with some emotion he could not identify. "It means 'the rich ones.' It is supposed to be very pretty." She wrapped her arms around her father's neck but her eyes were on Fargo. "Maybe we will build a castle there."

The count kissed her cheek and smiled down at her indulgently.

"Los Ricos," Fargo said slowly. "Nope, never heard of it," he lied.

Yeah, his instinct to keep his mouth shut about his destination had been right. Fargo turned about abruptly and went to fetch the kid's horse. As he led the boy's horse back toward the waiting group, he was sure he'd stumbled right into the middle of it.

Count Aznar sent his three men out to round up the horses. Fargo searched the rocks and found one other boy, shot by the travelers before he and Akando had arrived. Fargo swore to himself. What were these boys up to? He set out to search the area, wondering where Akando had gone. A hundred yards away, he spotted a bloody handprint, then bloodstains on rocks, droplets that led up to where a horse had been tethered. Then tracks leading away. Fargo followed them for a short distance and saw them joined by the prints of another horse.

So that's where Akando had gone. He'd probably noticed the ambushers were kids, just as Fargo had, and then followed a wounded one who was trying to escape. Fargo returned to the group, which had assembled near the low rock circle. Manrique was saddling up. He glared at Fargo. A deep red mark was visible on his jaw. It would turn into a helluva bruise.

Fargo took a swig from his canteen, then poured water into his hat and let the Ovaro drink.

"You are a very brave man, Senor Skye Fargo," Serena said, sidling up to him. Her shoulders were bare and lovely in the lowering sun, and the firm mounds of her breasts had a deep shadow between them. She smiled, kittenish again. "You are riding alone?"

Fargo suddenly felt on guard. He didn't want to

mention Akando. The less he told them, he decided, the better. He didn't trust the count and his men, or even Serena. They were all up to something. But what?

"I guess you could say that every man rides alone in El Diablo," Fargo said lightly.

"But what is your business?" she said. "It must be very interesting." She reached out one finger and lightly traced the line of buttons down the front of his shirt, her eyes on his chest. Her touch was electric and he wanted to seize her, bend her soft curves to his will. He could smell the musky odor of her, like heavy flowers but with lemons mixed in. "So strong." Her hand dropped to the butt of his Colt, which she touched lightly. Then she put her finger to her lips. "And I think, yes, I think this gun has killed many, many men." She glanced into his face again as if trying to read him. That dark gleam was behind her eyes again. "Yes, Senor Fargo, I think it must be very interesting business that brings you to El Diablo."

"Going from one place to the next," he said with a diffident smile. She was like a snake, a cougar, a cat.

"Well, senor," the count said, preparing to mount, "it has been a pleasure running into you. Thank you for your assistance in driving off those attacking peasants. And now, which way are you heading?"

"I think I'm going to tag along up to Los Ricos,"

Fargo said lightly. "Never been that way before. Sounds like an interesting place."

"But . . . but . . ." Hagan Crowley looked panicked, his pale face reddening.

"Shut up," the count snapped, his face betraying some emotion, like a wave of anger. Then it passed as he controlled his expression by putting on a tight smile. "Wonderful," he said, turning his horse about.

Manrique glared at Fargo.

"Wonderful," Serena repeated with her enigmatic smile. She swung onto her horse, a spirited stallion. From her seat and the way she held the reins, Fargo could tell she was an expert rider. They started off, with Manrique and the other man in the lead. Fargo brought up the rear, following Serena. She looked back from time to time, her long hair blowing in the wind like a wild horse's tail.

She was damned fine looking, Fargo thought. But something told him she had a black heart. Just like her father. Yeah, he'd stumbled right into it this time. Trouble had its way of finding him. And he was sure there was even more trouble ahead, up in the town of Los Ricos.

2

The seemingly endless land of El Diablo stretched before them, shimmering in the blasting heat of the sun. For two days, Fargo had ridden with the count and his daughter and their men. Their horses had walked mile after weary mile, their hooves breaking though the dry crust of alkali or clattering on the sunbaked stones.

For two days, Fargo had tried to figure out what the hell Spanish royalty was doing in the middle of this no-man's-land. But the count was unreadable—friendly and cordial, but wary. So was his daughter, Serena, who treated Skye alternately with warm interest and cool disdain. Manrique and the other man watched him as if they expected trouble. And Hagan Crowley, who chattered nonstop on the first day, got a bad case of sunburn when he neglected to wear a hat and turned sullen and quiet.

Fargo gave up trying to find out anything and withdrew into silence as they rode through the harsh land. He'd find out everything once they reached Los Ricos. The only thing he was certain of was that the count was up to no good. But whether it had something to do with what Gregorio had told the old monk remained to be seen.

Meanwhile, while they rode along, Fargo was constantly aware that Akando was following them. Occasionally, he would catch sight of a movement at the top of a tall cliff or see a slight smudge of dust against the distant horizon. Yes, the Apache was out there somewhere. But Fargo knew the Indian had also sensed something about the ambush situation that was not quite right. Undoubtedly Akando had watched and listened to what had happened from the cover of rocks and had the same questions he did. Who were those boys? Why were they trying to ambush Generalisimo Vito Ramirez? Why had Manrique shot the kid? And who was Count Aznar and his beautiful daughter? And the Apache had come to the conclusion that it was better for him to follow Fargo at a distance and to remain invisible. At least for now.

It was midafternoon when they came to the edge of a short cliff. Count Aznar, riding in the lead, raised his arm to call a halt and called out to his men in Spanish. Manrique and his cohort rode up and dismounted, pulling the tin cups from their saddles and filling them from the goatskin water bags for Aznar and his daughter.

Fargo dismounted and pulled out his canteen. He poured some water into his hat and held it for the pinto. The Ovaro was amazingly fresh, in better shape than the other mounts. As it drank,

Fargo looked out at the prospect. Ahead of them, the land was broken into cliffs and rock piles and shallow canyons. In the distance, sharp mesas gnawed the sky, and a dusty plain glimpsed between two hills looked tantalizingly like a cool ocean. But there was no water in this land. Here and there, beside the El Diablo trail, they had come across the bones of cattle that had strayed too far and the ribs of abandoned wagons from settlers who'd ventured the wrong way.

The Ovaro finished drinking and nuzzled him. Fargo took a swig from the canteen. There were only a few swallows left, he noticed. All along the El Diablo trail, the water holes had been nothing but cracked mud. Fargo put the hat back on his head, felt the droplets of cool water trickle down his neck, and walked toward the edge of the cliff where the count and Serena were looking out over the landscape below.

Fargo knew enough Spanish to understand that Serena was asking her father where the town lay. In answer, Count Aznar gestured toward the line of high mesas, cool blue against the far horizon, then noticed Fargo's presence beside them.

"Los Ricos is right there," he said in English, pointing to a spot along the mesas. He raised a brass eyeglass to one eye and began to survey the land.

Serena turned away from her father and toward Fargo and smiled, her dark eyes, fringed with long lashes, gleaming in the sunlight like black diamonds. Today she wore a leather riding skirt that accentuated her narrow waist and a man's white shirt, hardly buttoned. Through the thin cotton, he could see the swelling outline of her breasts and the hard points of her nipples.

"You will be glad to get to Los Ricos, Senor Fargo?" she asked him, smiling when she saw the direction of his gaze. She was in one of her friendly moods, he could see. With one hand, she idly played with the buttons on her shirt.

"I like the scenery," Fargo said, his eyes on her breasts. "Especially the mountains. Very picturesque. Makes me want to climb them." Serena smiled and licked her lips slowly with the pink point of her tongue.

"Too bad I'm just passing through Los Ricos," Fargo said with a shrug. "It's all the same to me."

"But then you will ride on, isn't that right?" Serena blinked her eyes at him and shook her long hair, which shone like black fire. "I will be very sorry to see you ride on. Very sorry."

Yeah, she was a damn flirt, Fargo thought, fed up with her on-again, off-again behavior. Any minute, he knew, she would turn into the ice queen.

"No you won't," Fargo said. "That's bullshit and you know it."

Serena's face registered a moment of disbelief at his words. The count lowered his eyeglass and glanced toward them. Then, like a sudden summer thunderstorm, Serena's face went dark with fury.

Fargo saw the slap coming and reached up to grab her arm. She struggled free of his grasp, then stomped off toward the horses.

Fargo laughed at her retreat and was surprised to notice the count chuckling under his breath.

"My daughter is not used to men who speak so directly to her," Aznar said.

"That's the way it is out here in the West," Fargo said. The count began looking through the eyeglass again while Fargo measured the distance to the mesas. Ten miles of broken land. They'd be there by nightfall.

"Hope there's some good water in Los Ricos," Fargo muttered, almost to himself.

"Sí, sí, there is water in Los Ricos," Count Aznar said, lowering the eyeglass. He took off his hat and ran his hand through his thick silver hair, but his eyes were still locked on the distance, which seemed to have a magical hold on him. "Water, so much water."

"You've been here before?" Fargo asked, watching the count's face. It was impossible to name the emotions he saw there—hope, longing, and something darker.

"Los Ricos, sí." The count's voice took on a dreamy quality. "Many years ago I was there. Many years. It is beautiful at Los Ricos, very beautiful. Golden sunsets, golden women, fruit, and beauty, there is everything . . ." Suddenly, he seemed to rouse himself, and then stopped speaking, shaking his head, as if he had said too much. Aznar quickly turned on his heel and walked toward his horse. He called out to his men in Spanish, and Fargo understood that he was telling them they would be in Los Ricos before dark.

The trail up to Los Ricos was so steep they dismounted and led the horses by foot. The rocky path was almost vertical, switching back and forth as it wound among white chalky cliffs and slopes of tumbled scree. As they climbed higher and higher, the broken land, striped with sunset shadows, fell away below them, and the pale sky, streaked with apricot and molten clouds, seemed to get closer and closer. Still they ascended, moving between white crumbling cliffs. Fargo saw that the town of Los Ricos was ideally situated. The path was so steep, treacherous, and narrow that a mere handful of men could defend it from any number of attackers. And yet they saw no men on guard. It was so inaccessible that probably few travelers ever went to the trouble of finding it.

Fargo wondered how Akando, following them, would scale the path without being seen. At last, when Fargo thought they must have come to the top of the mesa, they passed beneath the arch of a natural stone bridge and before him he saw the town of Los Ricos, washed with the last golden rays of the sun.

The small village covered the top of the narrow mesa and was built entirely of the white chalky stone. It was as if the houses had been built of snow and ice. On all sides, the cliff plunged straight down, leaving the narrow path the only way up. Through the narrow street, Fargo glimpsed an open square and the squat shape of a church with a bell tower, a pen filled with the woolly shape of sheep. But what he noticed most was that everywhere he looked were fruit trees and flowers, tomato vines and pepper plants, planted beside each house, and in pots in every window. The town was brimming over with lush green plants, like a Garden of Eden. And what amazed him even more was the sound of running water. He looked around and saw a narrow stone gutter running along the street, full of rushing water. Fargo bent down, filled his hat with it, and took a sip. Yes, it was sweet, tasting faintly of lime, but pure. He led the Ovaro over and let it drink.

Serena had stopped beside a tree of miniature apples. She reached up and picked one, laughing delightedly. Count Aznar, who was standing stock-still, looked down at the street with a strange expression on his face. Fargo wondered what the count was seeing, and he glanced down and saw that the street was paved with blocks of the same chalky stone that had been used to build the houses. Suddenly, he felt the count's eyes on him and he looked up with a smile.

"A beautiful town," Fargo said lightly.

Count Aznar nodded, a suspicious look in his eyes, then turned away and ordered Manrique and the other man to stable the horses. Hagan Crowley wandered as if dazed, looking around at everything, his skinny plaid-suited figure like a walking scarecrow. As he watched Crowley walk from flowerpot to flowerpot, poking at them with his long forked stick, the sun set and the golden light faded. The white town took on a pale blue color. Suddenly, Fargo saw a movement at the shutters of one of the houses and he realized someone was there watching from inside the house.

"Where are the people?" he muttered to himself, instantly aware that they had seen no one in this lush, perfect town of Los Ricos. Where were the citizens of this paradise? Serena was laughing and offering her father one of the small apples from a tree. Fargo walked past them, toward the square, watchful, wondering who lived in this strange place.

He had passed several houses when he saw a black-shawled figure hurrying down a street, an old woman nearly bent double. Fargo called out to her, greeting her in Spanish, but at the sound of his voice, she disappeared around a corner. He hurried after her, but when he turned the corner, there was no one to be seen. He heard the creak of a hinge. She had disappeared inside one of the houses. He continued toward the square.

In the center of the piazza rose a whitewashed fountain that gushed water. The small ditches radiated out in all directions, carrying the water away down the narrow streets. There was not a soul in sight. To one side of the square stood a squat whitewashed church with wooden doors. As he gazed at it, he saw the bell in the tower suddenly swing to one side and it began to peal. Eight times it rang, then stopped. Fargo sprinted across the square and pushed at the broad wooden doors.

Inside, the sanctuary was cool and smelled of incense. He glanced about in the dark shadows, then saw a figure in a dark robe and hood standing in the corner.

"Hello?" Fargo said.

The dark figure jumped, then began to run down the length of the church. Fargo gave chase and reached out just as they came to a low doorway. He grabbed a shoulder and spun the stranger around, then saw the face of a woman beneath the hood of her cloak. From what he could see of her she was very beautiful, her eyes very wide and frightened. She had full lush lips and a dark mole on her upper lip. She was panting with fright.

"Don't be afraid," Fargo said in Spanish. "I'm a friend." He could feel her body was tense, ready to dart away at any moment. "Who are you? What is your name?" he asked.

She shook her head violently, refusing to answer. There was no time to lose.

"Father Salvatore sent me," Fargo said. "I am looking for a man named Gregorio."

At the sound of the name, the woman stiffened, then nodded slowly. She seemed to relax. Fargo let go of her shoulder and she pointed through the door. They emerged in a small dirt courtyard at one side of the church. The wooden crosses stood in rows and each grave was decorated with dried flowers, ribbons, and leafy boughs. It was growing darker, the gold gone from the sky and the first stars twinkling overhead.

The silent woman led him to a cross and he saw Gregorio's name written on a rock in the center of a fresh mound. So, Gregorio was dead. The woman bent and moved some of the flowers on the grave. She looked up as if she were about to speak, her face twisted with pain, but just then the sound of gunfire and the shouts of men came from the street. In an instant, she had turned and disappeared through a low gate in the wall of the cemetery. Fargo hurried after her, more and more puzzled. What was this place? What the hell was going on?

The street was suddenly ringing with the sound of horses' hooves and the march of feet. Through the gathering twilight, Fargo saw the woman running down a side street. From the other direction, he saw marching toward him what seemed to be an entire army, bristling with bayoneted rifles.

In the front, mounted on a skittish brown, was a short, squat man in a tight white uniform. Even from this distance, Fargo knew from the drawings he'd seen in the newspapers that it was the generalissimo, Vito Ramirez, renowned throughout Mexico as a fierce opponent and harsh commander.

The generalissimo was famous for having virtually wiped out the bandidos and lawless marauders in this part of Mexico. Along the way, he'd also wiped out entire villages of Apaches just because they were Indians. In return for keeping law and order, everybody was supposed to house and feed his troops. There was also talk the generalissimo had pillaged and burned out some ranchers who didn't pay him proper tribute. And there were stories of how men who disobeyed him were treated worse than the Apaches. It was no wonder men called him the Iron Thumb.

Fargo stood beside the church wall in a shadow and watched the approach of the general, row on row of men marching behind him. They were just a few yards away when the commander caught sight of him. He reined in. The uniformed men behind him came to an abrupt halt.

"A man in Los Ricos! I have not seen this for a long time!" the generalissimo called out. Fargo wasn't sure he'd understood the Spanish right. Did the general mean he didn't recognize his face?

Suddenly, the general flicked his hand and four men dashed forward. It wasn't until they reached him that Fargo realized what they were up to. They were closing in like four hungry wolves for the kill.

In a flash, Fargo drew his Colt and fired, careful to just wing the first soldier, who fell back screaming and holding his elbow. As the second man closed in, Fargo swung his hand holding the Colt in a wide arc, catching the man across the face, snapping his neck around. He went down to his knees, then fell forward. Fargo spun about as he felt rather than saw the third one and lashed out with a kick that struck the man full in the belly, crunching his ribs. The man spun backward, falling against the wall and knocking himself out.

The fourth one jumped him from behind and Fargo felt the man's powerful arms suddenly lock around him. Fargo relaxed all his muscles for an instant, as if giving up, then suddenly bent his knees and pitched forward, curling up into a ball as the man turned a somersault over his head and landed on his back in the cobble street. Fargo leaped on him and held him down, but it was unnecessary. The man was out cold.

Fargo raised his Colt and pointed it straight at the general's chest. Immediately, the front line of the army troop knelt in perfect unison and there was a clatter as they brought their rifles into firing position. Fargo stared down the barrels of about two dozen rifles.

There was a long moment of silence. Fargo's finger was tight on the trigger of his Colt. There was no need for him to say that if anybody fired a bullet at him, the general himself would be dead in the next instant. The general knew damn well, but he didn't move a muscle. The soldier who had been winged crawled away and took cover.

"What the hell's going on?" Fargo called out. "You wanna send some more of your boys my way?"

"You speak *English!*" the general said, sounding delighted and completely ignoring the fact that

Fargo's pistol was aimed right at him. "A gringo! You are American, sí? And what a fighter!"

The generalissimo brought his horse forward at a slow walk, until he was only a few yards from Fargo. The Colt was trained on his chest. The troop knelt and stood, silent, disciplined, ready to fire.

"Do I know you?" the general said, peering down at him through the half dark. The general's face, with a thin black mustache and three chins, matched the rest of his stocky body. His white uniform was decorated with a double row of brass buttons and by fringed epaulets.

"Name's Skye Fargo. Now, what the hell's going on?" There was a murmur of voices as some of the troops recognized his name.

"I've heard of you!" the general said. "Famous man."

"I've heard of you, too," Fargo said.

This seemed to delight the general, who laughed heartily, leaning backward in his saddle. Finally, he wiped the tears from his eyes, and still chuckling, said, "I have always wanted to meet you, Senor Trailsman. But I didn't think it would be like this. My great apologies for this . . . this mess. We thought you were somebody else." Generalissimo Ramirez turned around to his troops and spoke in a low voice. Instantly, they snapped to attention, bringing their rifles up onto their shoulders. The front row got to its feet and they too stood at perfect attention. Fargo slowly lowered his Colt.

"Did you see this man fight?" the general called out to his men. "Now *that* is fighting! If I had a dozen men who could fight like this Senor Trailsman, I could get rid of all of you! Now, fall out, take your places for the first watch."

The troop dispersed, some groups moving quickly down the street, others retreating the way they had come. A soldier hurried forward with a small wooden platform and the general dismounted. He was so short and he rode such a large horse, a gigantic hulk of a bay, that dismounting would have been difficult without the stool. The soldier hurried away with it and the horse. General Vito Ramirez extended his hand to Fargo, who holstered his gun and shook.

"Please, Senor Fargo," the general said. "We will forget this mistake. You will be my guest at the cantina and we will drink together and tell stories." The general gestured to the far side of the square and they began walking. "And we will forget and forgive this little misunderstanding. Please."

Fargo nodded and smiled affably at the general, but he kept his thoughts to himself. Sure, he'd forgive. But forget? Never. The general had thought he was somebody else. But who? Who was he after? And why were General Vito Ramirez and Count Aznar meeting in Los Ricos? No, he wouldn't forget.

The cantina was just off the main square, a long, low building with lighted windows. The general pushed open the door and Fargo followed him.

Inside the whitewashed room were a dozen dark wooden round tables with stools. On one end of the room, an open stairway led up to a dark curtained door, and at the other was a rude bar, a counter made of hewn logs on which stood a row of stout glasses and a few bottles of white liquor. Behind the bar stood a frail old man, wiping glasses and looking nervous. A few of the tables were filled with some of the general's officers, who stood and saluted as he entered, then sat again.

"Welcome to the Los Ricos cantina," the general said, slapping Fargo on the back. "What'll it be?"

Fargo ordered a tequila and the general took the same. The fiery white cactus juice came with a fresh lime, a knife to cut it with, and a dish of salt. That was the Mexican way. They headed for a table in the corner. Fargo headed for the seat where he could sit with his back against the wall, and reached it just as the general did. They stood for an awkward moment, and then the general laughed and Fargo found himself joining in. If only to lull the general's suspicions.

"You are a cautious man," Ramirez said. "Like a general has to be. I like you, Senor Fargo," he said. Fargo moved a seat so that they could both keep watch on the room.

"Now, tell me what brings you to Los Ricos?" the general said. His eyes were bright with curiosity as they flicked once at Fargo, but the commander kept his gaze focused on his own hands as he began to cut the two limes into wedges.

Fargo told the tale of rounding up the cattle down south, leaving out any mention of Akando. No need to arouse the general's famous hatred of Apaches. As he drew out the long-winded tale, he wondered where Akando was. Lurking somewhere out around the city. And he also wondered where the count and his daughter had gone off to. Fargo drew out the story as long as he could, putting in every kind of detail about the battle with the bandidos and the geography of the ranch lands.

"That is all very interesting," the general said. He had just finished cutting up another lime and they were well into the second bottle of tequila. The general carefully arranged the lime wedges in rows. Then, taking the knife, he plunged it into the wooden table, and his gaze met Fargo's. "But you haven't told me why you are in Los Ricos."

"Neither have you," Fargo said with a smile.

The general smiled at that but his eyes were hard as stone. Fargo realized he'd made a mistake here. The last thing he wanted to do was to arouse suspicions that he had anything to hide. Fargo scratched his cheek, then took a long swig of the tequila. He could feel the burning liquid course through him and the room was slightly hazy. He wasn't drunk yet, but he was getting there. He dipped a wedge of lime in salt and bit into it, enjoying the clarifying burst of sharp citrus. The general had drunk just as much as he had, but from his appearance, he seemed cold sober. Fargo faked a hiccup, then rubbed his face as if he were feeling no pain.

"Actually," Fargo said, taking another swig and slurring his words a little, "actually, I stopped in here at old Los Ricos for some water," he said. He put down the glass a little too heavily and rubbed his face again, then straightened up in his chair as if trying to get himself under control. Yeah, he could do a damn good imitation of a drunk, he'd seen so many of 'em. "And I ran into some folks coming this way," Fargo added. "A Spanish guy, Count Aznar, and his daughter."

The general's face betrayed absolutely no emotion or recognition. His gaze was completely steady, his eyes never leaving Fargo's face. The man was good. Real good.

"You know 'em?" Fargo asked the general as he raised his glass to him.

The general nodded.

"Yeah," Fargo said. He faked another hiccup. "Now that was a test, you see. Because I know you know the count. He told me he was coming here to meet up with you."

"That's right," the general said, smiling. "So, I passed your little test."

"You did," said Fargo. He stared at the glass in his hand, shook his head as if trying to clear it, then shoved the glass away from him. Inside, he felt cold sober, but he knew the general was now convinced he was pretty drunk. And, from the looks of things, the general bought his story. The general filled his glass again and pushed it toward him. Fargo grinned and knocked it back in one gulp.

Just then, there was a flurry at the front door and a group came in. Among them were Manrique and Hagan Crowley. They looked around and Manrique registered surprise and suspicion to see Fargo sitting with the general, but he didn't come over. Fargo plied the general with a few innocent-sounding questions like how large his troop was and where they were heading now, which the general managed to deflect. He was a hard man to get information out of. A few minutes later, there came the sound of a flute playing, not very well. It seemed to be a signal, because at the sound of the first few notes, all the men in the bar hushed at once and turned around to face the curtained door at the head of the wooden stairs.

A moment later, the curtains parted and a woman stepped through them. She was very tall and wore her hair piled high under a white lace mantilla. Her purple dress was cut so low that the dark, erect nipples of her small pushed-up breasts were visible over the white lace neckline. The soldiers whistled, beat their glasses on the tables, and called out at her as she moved slowly down the stairs. Another woman appeared in the doorway. She was wearing red, her very rounded figure packed tight into her dress. Her long dark hair fell in waves around her shoulders, and the bodice of her gown was made of black lace through which

Fargo could see her very full breasts. She blew kisses toward the men as she walked slowly down the stairs. The third woman was dressed in yellow, her gown unlaced and her pale breasts and pink nipples completely exposed. She paused at the top of the stairs and smiled down at the men, then licked one finger and touched the nipple of one breast. The soldiers went wild as the women walked slowly among the tables, stopping to talk to the men, who had a hard time keeping their hands off the goods. A lieutenant pulled a wad of bills out of his pants and grabbed the arm of the woman in yellow, tugging her toward the staircase. Suddenly, a dark figure stepped forward from beside the bar. Fargo had not noticed her there before. She was a commanding figure, severe, dressed in a plain black dress with a high neck and long sleeves. Her dark hair was pulled back in a single long braid. Even from across the room, Fargo recognized her. It was the woman from the cemetery.

The lieutenant handed her the bills and ran up the stairs behind the woman in yellow. They were quickly followed by the two other women with two more soldiers, who each paid the woman in black. So she was the local madam.

"Nice women in Los Ricos, eh?" the general said.

"Oh, yeah," Fargo said. He licked his lips, scratched his head, and took another drink. The bottle of tequila was almost empty. The general raised his arm and summoned the woman in black. She approached slowly, her eyes downcast. When she drew near, Fargo realized she was trembling.

She glanced up into Fargo's face and registered surprise. Her mouth fell open. Fargo felt the general stiffen with suspicion.

"Senor, are you . . . are you the man . . ."

"Yeah," Fargo said, sloshing his drink as he put it down. "Yeah, I'm the guy that pinched you in the street this afternoon. You got a nice ass, lady. I'll pinch it again if you just turn around."

The woman looked completely taken aback and confused. She shook her head from side to side as she backed away and the general called after her for more tequila. She hastened to the bar and sent the old man over with the third bottle of tequila.

The general poured him another full drink and took only a splash for himself. Hell, he'd have to slow down the drinking now, Fargo realized, because the room really was beginning to sway a little. The general wagged his finger in Fargo's direction.

"Senor Fargo, I am surprised at you," the general said. "I expected a man who could hold his liquor."

"Oh, I'm sober," Fargo protested, sitting up straighter. "Yeah, real sober."

"And someone must teach you the manners of Los Ricos," the general went on. "That woman is named Ignacia. She is in mourning. So you are not supposed to bother her." The general glanced in her direction. "Even though I would like to." His gaze lingered on her as if he could undress her from across the room.

"Mourning?" Fargo asked innocently, sucking on the lime. "Who died?"

"Her father," the general snapped. "Used to run this cantina. Stupid man. Very stupid."

Fargo realized it must be Gregorio. He was about to ask about Gregorio when there was a flurry of activity by the entrance. Count Aznar and Serena had arrived. Tonight she was wearing a green silk gown, cut low, and a dark lace mantilla that accentuated the ebony sheen of her long hair. The count wore a gray silk cape that matched his silver hair. The general stood, as if at attention. Fargo got heavily to his feet and pretended to sway as he stood. Yeah, he was feeling no pain, but he wasn't drunk. The count spotted them and escorted his daughter through the tables.

The general bowed to the count and kissed Serena's hand, then gestured for them to sit. Fargo touched the brim of his hat, then belched for Serena's benefit.

"He's quite drunk," the general said under his breath in Spanish.

"Disgusting man," Serena replied quietly, also in Spanish. Fargo pretended not to take any notice.

"So, we must talk," the general said loudly in English, clearly for Fargo's benefit. "I want to hear all about our family."

Fargo was surprised. He glanced up at the count and the general.

"You two brothers?" he asked, pointing from one to the other. There was a vague resemblance in the eyes and forehead, even though the count was tall and the general was so squat.

"Cousins," the count said with an oily smile. "Yes, we have so much family news to catch up on, Vito. Perhaps Ignacia will find a quiet room for us. Come, Serena." The three of them rose and the general summoned Ignacia, who refused to look in Fargo's direction. She pulled a ring of keys from her waist and handed one to the old bartender, who started to lead the three of them in the direction of the stairs.

Damn. He needed to find out what they were going away to talk about. And he needed to speak with Ignacia, too. But how? Suddenly, Fargo rose from his seat and stood swaying from side to side.

"Hey, you can't just go off like that," he bellowed. "Come over here, you." He made a grab for Serena's arm, but purposely missed and stumbled forward. He caught the edge of a round table with one hand and looped his other arm around Ignacia's waist. As they fell, he pulled her close, until his mouth was at her ear. They hit the floor and rolled, the table crashing down on top of them. For effect, Fargo kicked over a couple of chairs.

"I'm not drunk," he said into Ignacia's ear as they were rolling over on the floor. "Only pretending. I need to talk to you about Gregorio. Now."

52

The place was in an uproar. Serena screamed and the general shouted orders. Several officers came running and set the table upright, disentangled him from Ignacia, and pulled him to his feet. Now for the tricky part, Fargo thought as he lashed out with his fists ineffectually. Suddenly, he pitched forward as if to strike one of the soldiers, but instead he dove to the floor. As soon as he landed, he lay still and let his body go limp.

"So, this is the great Senor Gringo," the general said in Spanish. Fargo felt the general kick his ribs, and not lightly, either. It took all of his will not to react to the burst of pain that radiated along one side. "He is out cold, the stupid. From his reputation, I expected a hero. Somebody brave, strong. A warrior. Sure he can fight. But he is a drunken fool. And not very smart, either. Lock him up."

"No, no," Fargo heard Ignacia interrupt. "I will have him carried upstairs to a room where he can sober up. Leave him to me."

The general didn't even bother to respond, and Fargo heard the general, the count, and Serena ascending the staircase. Then it took three soldiers to carry his limp body up the stairs, and they did it none too gently. Ignacia led the way, giving them instructions, until at last he felt himself being thrown like a sack of grain onto a feather bed. The door closed and all was quiet, then he heard a slight rustle in the room. Someone was there.

Fargo waited a minute, and then slowly opened his eyes.

Ignacia stood over him, looking down with concern. She crossed the room, locked the door, and returned with a glass of water. Fargo sat up and drank down the water. Yeah, he was a little high, but okay. The room was furnished simply with a large wooden bedstead and cupboard and a couple of leather chairs. Ignacia sat down slowly on a chair and Fargo sat on the edge of the bed. He looked her over. Despite the plainness of her black dress, which covered everything, she was more beautiful than any of the other women in the cantina. Her dark eyes were like a doe's.

"Speak English?"

"Yes."

"Gregorio was your father?" he said.

Ignacia nodded.

"He told Father Salvatore that the whole village was going to die. Do you know what he meant?"

Ignacia considered the question for a moment. She nodded no at first, then yes.

"I . . . I know but I do not know," she started to explain. "The way my father knew. It is nothing definite. But, yes, I know we will all die."

"Who will kill you?" Fargo asked. "The general?"

"Of course," she said. "There is no one who can stop him if he wants to kill you. There is no one to help us."

"What about your men?" Fargo asked. "Can't the

54

men of the village fight together? It would not take very many to defend this village."

Ignacia's eyes filled with tears.

"Men?" she said. "You see men in Los Ricos? We have not had men here for many, many years." Fargo realized that she was right. He had not seen one man, except the very old bartender. In fact, he had hardly seen anybody.

"Where are they?"

"The general takes them away," Ignacia said bitterly. "The conscription. He can take any man he finds to fight in his army. At first we hoped to see the men again when the army came back to the village. But the men of Los Ricos, none of them come back. All of them are dead. Why? I do not understand. And the general, he tries to take away the boys, too. So the mothers, they make the boys run away to the mountains."

Fargo nodded, remembering the boys who ambushed the count, thinking he was Generalissimo Vito Ramirez. Now it all made sense. The boys were from Los Ricos, hiding in the hills. Unfortunately, what the general was doing wasn't illegal in Mexico. The army could seize any man and make him come along and fight for as long as they wanted him to. And deserters were shot in the face.

"But why is Count Aznar here in Los Ricos? He and the general have some kind of plan."

"This I do not know anything about," Ignacia said.

"Where are they?" he asked. "I must hear what they are talking about. Is that possible?"

"Maybe," Ignacia said, but he saw the wave of fear cross her features. He could easily read her face. If the general caught her betraying him, he would have her shot. Or worse. Mourning or not. "What will you . . . pay me?" Ignacia said. Fargo was surprised at the question.

"What's your price?"

"Please, senor," she said. She was trembling again. "Please just get me out of Los Ricos."

"Yeah," Fargo said. "I'll do that for you. You have my word."

Ignacia put her finger to her lips and moved quietly to the door. She unlatched it and then peered down the hall. Fargo could hear the raucous voices of soldiers singing from the great room downstairs, and also a woman laughing from a nearby room, as well as the rhythmic sound of bedsprings squeaking.

Fargo followed Ignacia as she moved out into the hallway. They had nearly reached the end when one of the doors sprung open and a soldier's voice swore in Spanish. Ignacia opened a door and they slipped inside just in time. They were in a small narrow room that functioned as a storage closet. Fargo could hear voices on the other side of the wall but they were muffled and he couldn't make out the words. On pegs on both walls hung various gowns, fringed shawls, lace shawls, huge cages of hoopskirts, and voluminous white petticoats. Ignacia moved through the narrow path between the silks and satins and then stopped, reaching between the dresses to pull them back. Behind them was a knothole in the pine board wall. He peered into it and saw a small room with a round table where the count, the general, and Serena sat. The words were still indistinct. Fargo put his ear to the knothole.

"Well, that about wraps it up," the general said. "I know exactly what to do and when." They were speaking in Spanish and Fargo had to struggle to keep up with their words.

"And of course when the villa is finished, you and your men can make Los Ricos your headquarters."

"The capital of the territory," the general said enthusiastically.

"But what about this Skye Fargo?" the count asked.

"He is an idiot," the general replied. "Believe me, I sat with him all night. Stupid, stupid."

Fargo, his ear pressed against the knothole, noticed that Ignacia had found another and was also listening, her ear against the wall. Her face, just inches from his, was thoughtful.

"I wouldn't be too sure," Serena said. "I don't trust him."

"Fine, my dear," the count put in. "Your instincts about men are always right. So, if he doesn't just leave in a day or two—"

"I'll take care of him," the general said.

"Meanwhile, tomorrow Crowley will find it," the count said. "Just think, what we have been waiting for all these years. Your men will keep everybody away, right?"

"Of course," the general said. "They have their orders. And if it is what we think it is, we will shoot everybody. It is easier that way. No questions later about who owns what. And it will be so easy to make it look like Jorge Gomez. My men like to do that."

Fargo remembered the men lying in El Diablo with their tongues ripped out. So, it was the general making it look like Gomez. It was all part of his plan. Fargo heard the crinkle of paper.

"Now if we can just figure this out." It was the count speaking. Fargo looked through the hole again and saw the count holding a small slip of paper. "This is the key. It must be in some kind of code. *Golden fine honey,*" he read.

"That must be the mother lode," the general said.

"Or gold coins," Serena put in.

"But what does this mean, *everybody is blind*? It must mean something." The count sounded exasperated.

"Never mind," the general said, "if you think this man can find it."

"In Barcelona, we saw him find the Countess Allende's lost gold necklace in an almond grove," Serena said. "It was amazing. Oh, yes, he's very good."

"Well, then," the general said, "until tomorrow."

Fargo and Ignacia waited in silence as they listened to the three leaving the room and descending the staircase into the noisy cantina. When he was sure they were well out of hearing, he straightened up. Ignacia did as well, looking preoccupied.

"Golden fine honey. Everybody is blind," she repeated. "I know those words from somewhere. But—I can't remember."

They returned quietly to the other room. Once the door had been closed behind them, Fargo said, "Thank you for what you've done. I'll figure out a way to get you out of here in the next couple of days." He thought of Akando, who could be helpful—he if could figure out a way to signal him. There was a roar of laughter and applause from down below. "Maybe you'd better get back down there," Fargo said. "Will it look suspicious if you're gone too long?"

"I guess you're right," Ignacia said. She started to leave and then turned back to him.

"I don't even know your name," she said. He smiled at her.

"So you don't," he said. "It's Skye Fargo."

Her face changed suddenly, twisting into an expression that looked like pain and then became grief. The tears filled her eyes and then brimmed over and ran down her cheeks as she stood with one hand on the door, weeping silently yet heartbreakingly. Fargo crossed to her and locked the door, took her in his arms, and led her to the bed.

The tears would not stop coming and her lips trembled. Suddenly, he took her in his arms and she began to sob. He'd seen it happen before, women who'd been brave for so long, who'd bottled up their fear. And then it would all break loose.

"It's all right," he said, taking her onto his lap. "You're safe now. Everything will be all right." He held her for a long time, his arms wrapped around the warm curves of her beneath the black silk of her dress, inhaling the spicy odor of her skin, her hair. Beneath the warm softness of her, he felt himself harden with desire, imagining the smoothness of her skin, her legs, what was between them. She must have felt him stir. He stroked her hair. Gradually, her sobs subsided and she sat very still, as if waiting for him to make a move. No, this one had to be handled differently.

Long minutes passed and he felt the hot rod of his wanting throbbing to be inside her. Still, he waited, and then, shyly, she took his hand and put it to her warm, soft breast. She lifted her tear-stained face and gazed into his eyes.

"You sure?" he said.

"I know I am safe now," she said. "Yes, yes, Skye Fargo, I want you. Please."

3

Ignacia was warm in his arms, her weight against him heavy, soft. He nuzzled her neck, seeking the silken skin above the high black collar of her mourning dress.

"You sure?" he murmured again.

In answer, she turned her face up toward him, her mouth willing, wanting, her eyes dark with desire. He kissed her, deeply, and she opened to him as his tongue explored the sweetness of her, feeling her hands stroking the hard muscles of his broad back. He slowly moved his hand to cover her high, full breast. Her breathing quickened; she panted beneath the constraining silk of her gown. Fargo began to undo the buttons down her front, until he could see the black lace camisole underneath. Then he slipped his hand inside and held one warm breast, overflowing his palm, and stroked the soft nipple, felt it harden to a point beneath his fingers.

"Oh, yes, Skye," she murmured.

Ignacia leaned back and slipped out of the dress, then pulled it down over her hips, along with her pantaloons. As he sat on the edge of the bed, she stood shyly for a moment before him in the black lace camisole, the straps slipping off her smooth shoulders. He let his gaze linger on her honey-colored thighs, the black lace stockings held by garters, and the dark triangle between her legs. Suddenly, she reached up and loosed the braid in her hair, shaking it out until it fell around her shoulders like a dark mane. Her huge dark eyes were soft in the flicker of the lamplight and she was smiling. She looked so different from the woman he had seen in the cemetery.

Fargo kicked off his boots, stripped off his shirt, and lay back on the quilted bed.

"Beautiful," he said appreciatively, holding out his hand to her. She smiled and came to him and he pulled her onto the bed.

As she lay beside him, he let his hands slowly explore the extravagant curve of her narrow waist, lifting the camisole to look at her breasts, the smooth round hills crowed by crinkled and erect nipples and large brown areolae. As he leaned over her and kissed her slowly, beginning with her flat belly and moving slowly upward toward her breasts, she reached down and began to stroke the fabric of his Levi's, tight over the hard swelling of his eager cock.

"So large," she whispered as she began to unbutton his pants.

He took a nipple into his mouth, flicking it with his tongue, and heard her gasp at the same moment. He moved his hand downward, suddenly covering her warm fur, feeling her wetness beneath his fingers as he explored the slick folds of her and inserted a finger, then two, up into her.

"Ah, ah, *sí, sí*! Skye, ah . . ."

He felt the shudder shake her body thoroughly as she tightened, her hips suddenly bucking beneath his hand, her body uncontrollable. He rubbed her again, finding the hard swollen button of her desire. She lifted her hips off the bed in a spasm of ecstasy. He kissed her mouth and she sucked eagerly on his tongue, breathing hard.

"Ah! Ah!" Ignacia tossed back and forth, and he could tell she was about to come. She fumbled with his trousers and slipped her hand inside, and he felt her grasp his huge swollen rod.

"Yes, yes," she breathed. "Please."

He slipped his Levi's off as she opened her legs to him and he paused to savor the sight of her, the black lace stockings and garters, the circle of glistening fur, the pink wet folds and the dark opening, his dark cock sliding slowly into her, up into the tightness of her.

He ground into her, lifting her hips up toward him, forgetting everything but the musk-scented woman beneath him, the warm welcoming tightness of her as he plunged in and out, deeper and deeper, his cock throbbing with pleasure. She contracted at once, coming in waves, giving herself totally to the pleasure of it, her face contorted with euphoria.

"Oh, *Dios*, yes . . . Skye," she muttered as she slowed, the orgasm over. Fargo took his time, slowing, stroking in and out of her, long delicious plunges, his manhood pulsating. Yeah, he wanted this one to last a while. Ignacia moved under him now like an ocean wave, rising and falling with his movements. She smiled up at him and he kissed along her forehead, then her mouth, sweet.

"You're like a volcano," he said, continuing to stroke inside her. He could feel her squeezing him with her muscles, tightening around his penis.

"My name means fire," Ignacia said with a smile. She reached down through their legs and suddenly grasped his balls, stroking him. His cock wanted to explode; he could feel the pressure, the explosion coming on. He moved his hand downward, sliding it between them to touch her button, pushing into her as he plunged, harder and harder. She lifted beneath him, grinding her hips, calling out inarticulately as he could feel her getting ready to come again.

"*Sí! Sí!*" she cried out as her hips lifted up and he felt the shudder overtake her. His cock was hot as molten lava and he felt the explosion gathering, building, until he let it go, shooting, streaming up into her darkness, again and again, deeper into her shuddering body. Finally he slowed, and then stopped. He lay covering her, kissing her gently, feeling the rise and fall of their breathing as it slowed.

"Fire," he said to her. "You are made of fire."

Ignacia smiled sleepily up at him, her dark eyes heavy. He rolled off her and pulled the quilt over them, holding her close to him as she fell into a light sleep.

He turned the oil lamp down to a mere glow. Ignacia snuggled next to him. She was beautiful asleep, like a little girl, her hair strewn all around her, her hands curled beneath her head. She'd had a helluva time of it. The death of her father, the threat from General Vito Ramirez and his men, knowing that the town was doomed in some mysterious way, and no men here to protect the women of Los Ricos. The voices of men, laughing and shouting, and the clink of glasses and bottles filtered up from the cantina downstairs.

But his thoughts were full of what he and Ignacia had overheard of the conversation between the general, the count and Serena. The count had a piece of paper in his pocket that he said was in some kind of a code—something about golden honey and everybody being blind. And Ignacia had seemed to recognize the words but couldn't place them. If only he could get a look at the piece of paper. Maybe that would tell him why Count Aznar and Serena had come all the way from Spain to meet up with General Vito Ramirez in Los Ricos.

One thing he knew for sure. They were looking for something, and when they found it, they were going to kill everybody. They'd said as much. And they'd cut out their tongues to make it look like the work of Jorge Gomez and his gang. It was diabolical, but how could he single-handedly stop a whole troop armed to the teeth? He wished he could talk it over with Akando. And he wondered where the Apache was hiding out. Probably he was keeping an eye out on the mesa, waiting for word from Fargo. The beginning of a plan began to form in Skye's mind.

Ignacia's eyes fluttered open and for a moment she looked puzzled, then she relaxed and smiled up at him.

"That was wonderful, Skye Fargo," she said. "You are a very great lover. I have heard stories like that and now I know to believe them."

He kissed her lightly.

"I promised I'd get you out of Los Ricos," he said. "I think I can manage . . ."

"No," Ignacia said. She sat up and pulled the quilt around her. "No, I have changed my mind. This is my home. Now that you are here, Skye Fargo, I think the town will be saved."

He wished he had her confidence. General Ramirez and his men were well trained, a disciplined troop used to fighting, used to the terrain of El Diablo. How the hell could he overcome them?

"I guess you will be leaving in the morning," Ignacia said.

"What gives you that idea?" he replied.

"You heard what they said, the general and that count. They will kill you too if you do not leave tomorrow. They are afraid of you."

"But how can I save Los Ricos if I leave?" he asked her with a smile. The question had been bothering him, too. Once he left the mesa, it would be impossible to return. The high, narrow path could be easily guarded by just a few of the general's troops. And no matter how well he and Akando could ride and shoot, they would never be able to get back into the town. And in his absence, who knew what the general might do to the few townspeople left. He'd find a way to stay. "No," he said aloud. "I have to remain here in Los Ricos."

"But—"

Fargo interrupted her protest by putting his finger to her lips.

"You can do one thing for me," he said to her. "See if you can get your hands on that piece of paper Count Aznar had last night. I want to take a look at it."

Ignacia agreed to try, and wordlessly they got up and began to dress. Ignacia combed her hair and braided it again. As he was putting on his shirt, silver glinted as something fell out of the pocket and hit the floor. Fargo bent to retrieve it.

"Do you recognize this?" he asked Ignacia, holding up the silver chain with the strange turquoise turtle pendant. She stared at it, her eyes wide.

"Where did you get this?"

"Off the neck of a man lying dead about ten miles west of here," Fargo said. "A man and a boy. Their tongues cut out. Looked like the Gomez gang, but now I think maybe General Ramirez did it." Ignazia nodded slowly and thoughtfully, her dark eyes troubled. He could read fear in her face and something else . . . fury? "So what is this turtle?"

Ignacia had her mouth open to answer him when a knock came at the door, urgent, insistent. From down below, Fargo heard the loud voices of men and angry shouting. Ignacia, buttoning the high neck of her black dress, waved him behind a low screen standing in one corner. She approached the door and unlocked it. The old bartender, frail and frightened looking, stepped inside. He pulled nervously at his scraggly white hair.

"Senorita, *por favor*," he said. He went on to tell her that the men were having a dispute over one of the girls and couldn't she please come to settle it. She replied that she would be down in a moment, then closed the door behind the old man. With her severe black dress buttoned high and her braided hair, she looked so imperious and commanding, so different from the woman he had held in his arms a short time before.

"Do you want me to come with you?" Fargo asked.

"I think it is better if you stay here," Ignacia said. "I will say you are still out cold with the alcohol." She smiled suddenly. "You are a good actor, Skye Fargo, because I really believed you, and I have seen many drunk men. Stay here in this room for the night. For now, I must go."

Fargo kissed her lightly and she let herself back out into the hallway. He locked the door behind her, then paced up and down in the room for a while, listening to the voices down below. Within minutes, the dispute died down. Clearly, Ignacia had the respect of the general's troops. He continued pacing, frustrated, his mind whirling. He blew out the lamp and crossed to the window and opened it wide, leaned out, and looked down into the streets of Los Ricos.

It was well after midnight and the stars gleamed overhead in the clear air. The white chalky buildings of Los Ricos glowed in the faint starlight and the calming sound of running water reached his ears. Here and there, a few drunken soldiers staggered up the deserted streets. But he could also see others of the troop stationed at the corners of buildings. As he watched, a group of five came marching down the center of the street and disappeared in the other direction. Yeah, some of the men were off duty and making the most of it. But the rest were on guard, disciplined, ready for anything at a moment's notice.

He wondered how the Ovaro was. Earlier, he had paid the old bartender to make sure his horse was curried and stabled properly, and the old man had assured him it had been done. For a moment, he was tempted to climb out of the window and have a look around. But then he realized that if he was spotted, the whole game would be up. No, everything depended on General Ramirez and Count Aznar believing that he had a weakness for booze, that he was what he said he was. Fargo realized he was going to have to pretend to be another kind of man altogether. Only then could he stay in Los Ricos. Only then could he stay alive. He undressed again and lay down on the bed, but sleep was slow in coming.

"Attention!"

The rows of men snapped to attention, their tan jackets ablaze with brass buttons, the morning sunlight gleaming on the long barrels of their rifles. They were drawn up in battle formation in the main square, doing drill maneuvers, all aiming at the facade of the church. A lieutenant was shouting the commands in Spanish, while the rotund figure of General Vito Ramirez, the man they called the Iron Thumb, rode back and forth on his tall bay. Fargo could tell that nothing escaped his keen eye. But so far, the general had pretended not to notice him standing in front of the cantina, watching the drill.

"Aim! Fire! Fire! Fire!"

The earsplitting retort of dozens of rifles exploded and echoed off the white walls of Los Ricos. The white stucco wall of the church was obscured by a shower of splinters and dust. When it cleared, the wall was revealed to be badly scarred by the gunfire, densely pocked where the bullets had hit. Any enemy standing in front of the troop's furious fusillade wouldn't have a hope in hell of surviving.

"Fall out for combat drill!" the lieutenant shouted

again in Spanish. The troops broke their firing ranks and paired off around the square. The men began to practice bayonet lunges and defensive tactics, using the butts of their rifles as clubs, blocking other blows using the barrel. They were damned good, Fargo could see, well schooled in the kind of close in fighting that was the downfall of many army troops he'd seen.

There was one soldier standing off to the side who did not find a sparring partner. Seeing his chance, Fargo grabbed up a rifle that had been leaning against the wall and approached the man.

"Práctica?" Fargo said.

The young soldier, whose face was clean-shaven and seemed to be cut from granite, had cold black eyes and was built like a grizzly bear. He glanced at the lieutenant standing nearby. The officer shrugged his approval.

Fargo let the young man make the first move. He stood still, gripping the rifle with both hands, seemingly relaxed, but with every muscle in his body alert, ready. The big man circled warily. He lunged forward with his bayonet, but Fargo easily repelled it, and the soldier circled him again.

"What's your name?" Fargo asked him in Spanish.

The soldier registered surprise.

"Nesto," he answered, but at that moment Fargo struck out with his rifle, suddenly diving forward and sideways, catching the man's booted foot with his bayonet. Just as he thought, Nesto struck out defensively, throwing himself off balance, and Fargo thrust sideways with his rifle. Nesto's feet went out from under him and he hit the dust. As Fargo hit the ground, he swept his arm sideways and caught the rifle barrel, wrenching it from the soldier's grip. He tucked his feet under him and came up, holding both rifles. Nesto got to his feet, his granite face turned even harder, his black eyes spitting fury. He beat the dust from his uniform.

Without looking around, Fargo knew he'd attracted the general's attention. Good, his plan was working just fine. He tossed the rifle back to Nesto.

"Care to try again?" Fargo asked. Nesto did not respond, but his eyes were eloquent, like the dark barrels of two rifles. Loaded rifles. This time, Nesto did not move, trying to use Fargo's strategy, trying to get Fargo to make the first lunge. Fargo began walking slowly around the young soldier, dragging his rifle carelessly behind him in the dust. All around them, the other soldiers had stopped their practice and had turned to watch the two of them.

Fargo suddenly brought the rifle up, jumping a foot toward Nesto and shouting loudly. The soldier took a swing at him but he missed, and Fargo pulled back immediately, continuing his taunting circling. Again and again he feinted, shouting, pulling up as if to strike but not following through. It was like a game of cat and mouse, and after the fifth time, Fargo could see that Nesto was tiring of it, impatient to get his licks in, his anger rising. Yes, rage was the fighter's enemy and friend. It could cloud the mind or it could focus the body. Depended on how a man handled it.

Fargo feinted again, ready for Nesto to strike, knowing the big man would take a step too far. And he did. This time, the big man thrust upward with his bayonet, a move designed to flip the rifle out of Fargo's hands. Fargo let it go and the gun went flying up into the air, and just as Nesto came for him to knock him down, Fargo shifted his weight to one foot and gripped Nesto's rifle, and using all his weight, pulled it downward. The point of the bayonet stuck in the dust, and Nesto, carried by his forward momentum, flipped up over the gun, landing on his back. Fargo kicked his hand off the rifle and took it up, then pointed the bayonet at Nesto's throat.

"Remarkable! Really remarkable!" Fargo heard General Vito Ramirez say. The commander sat on his horse a short distance away.

Nesto got to his feet, his eyes sullen, and Fargo handed the soldier his rifle back, then offered his hand.

"No hard feelings," Fargo said as he shook the young man's hand. But Nesto did not repeat the words, only stared at him with fury.

"That was remarkable," the general said again. He brought his horse up alongside as Fargo beat the dust from his hat and put it on again.

"And you got yourself a fine troop of men here, General," Fargo said, returning the compliment.

General Ramirez sat on his tall horse looking down at him for a long moment. The sun glittered on the double row of brass buttons down his chest and on his gold epaulets. His thick face with its triple chins was unreadable, but Fargo could read what was in his eyes. Curiosity. Suspicion. Now it was time to go into the act, he realized.

"Guess I owe you an apology," Fargo said. He pulled his hat off his head and ran his fingers through his hair. "For last night. Guess I was pretty drunk. Can't remember what I said or did. Can't remember much of anything. That cactus juice never does sit too well with me."

The general sat still, looking down at him for a moment, saying nothing. The troop went back to their practice drills. Fargo scratched his head again, as if nervous. The general started his horse walking down the street, and Fargo walked alongside.

"Well, the other thing I was going to ask you is if you got any work needs doing. Trail kind of work. You know, that's my specialty." Fargo realized he was laying it on real thick, but he had to convince the general he was hard up. And that he was a weak man but trustworthy.

"Yes, I have heard your reputation," the general said stiffly. He didn't stop his horse, but they kept going down a deserted side street. It was damned stupid talking to a short man on a tall horse, Fargo thought. Vito Ramirez probably felt better looking down on him for a change.

"You see, General, I'm kind of hard up for cash right now," Fargo lied. "Real hard up. And I'd do anything for some work. Maybe even if you got some soldiering or something."

As the general glanced down at him, Fargo saw his face slowly change, an idea formulating in his eyes. He brought the bay to a halt.

"You need the money, eh?" the general said. "I can understand a man who needs money." There was a long pause as Vito Ramirez looked across the rooftops of Los Ricos and into the dry desert of El Diablo, which lay for a hundred miles in every direction.

"What if I had a shipment, a wagon train, that I needed to get to Sante Fe in two weeks' time? I supply the men to guard it, you lead."

"That's easy," Fargo said. "But you got to go through Apache territory. They watch those trails like vultures."

At the mere mention of his sworn enemies, General Ramirez's face went stony, and Fargo could read in his expression the hatred that had made the Iron Thumb the scourge of the Apaches. For some reason, the general hated the tribe more than anything else, and he never passed up an opportunity to brutally butcher any Apache he found.

"Let us say that I wanted to stay off the trails and blaze a new route to Sante Fe," the general said. "A new trail that the Apaches would not know about. One that the U.S. Army wouldn't know about either."

"That's my specialty," Fargo said. "Just costs you a little more. But I know that country like the back of my hand. There are canyons there that aren't on anybody's map. We could get through that country in two weeks, give or take a day. No problem. Let's say a thousand pesos and you got me."

The general nodded slowly but did not smile.

"You are an interesting man, Senor Fargo," he said. "A great fighter. That I have seen. A man of great strength and cunning. But also a man with great weakness." Ramirez looked back toward the square where his troop was still practicing.

"In the military, I have learned that every man has his weakness. But I use each man for his strength. You have the problem with tequila, no? But this is balanced by what you can do for me— get this shipment to Sante Fe."

"Sure," Fargo said. "Sure. You meet my price, I'll work for you."

"Agreed," said General Ramirez.

"When do we leave?"

"A while yet," the general said. "A week at the most." he paused for a long moment. "Don't you even want to know what we are transporting?"

"None of my business," Fargo said with a shrug. Hell, yes, he was curious to know what the general and the count had going on. But he had to keep playing the part of the mercenary, the man who did anything for money, no matter what it was. "I don't care a goddamn what my customers are up to. Never did. Long as I get paid, I don't ask questions. A man lives longer that way."

"Then we understand one another," the general said, smiling for the first time. "Yes, I think we understand each other very well. You will remain in Los Ricos for the next week, until we leave with the shipment. These are my orders. That is all."

The general turned his bay about and headed for the square. Fargo watched him go. Yeah, so far so good. He'd managed to allay the general's suspicions and got himself hired to boot. Now he could keep an eye on everything going on in Los Ricos.

For now, he'd have a look around and see the town in the daylight. For the next hour, he familiarized himself with the white stone streets of the mesa-top village. It was every bit as beautiful as it had seemed the day before. Down each street ran a small gutter of clear, cold water. Fruit trees planted in pots hung heavy with fruit, and flowers grew everywhere, spilling out of window boxes. Nevertheless, he could see that some of the plants were not so well cared for, and vines had overgrown some of the houses as if the inhabitants no longer cared. On nearly every street, there were soldiers standing guard. All the windows were shuttered and the doors were closed. Several times, Fargo caught sight of a woman or a small child, all dressed in black, hurrying down a street. But as soon as they spotted him, they seemed to melt away, disappearing into a door that he would find bolted shut when he tried it.

Once, when there were no soldiers in sight, he followed a woman and called out a couple of times in Spanish that he was a friend and wanted to talk, but then realized he would probably just get her in trouble, as well as make the general suspicious, and he let her go.

On the far side of the village, he came to a miniature square. There in the center he saw two oxen yoked to a spindle. They walked around and around while a small boy poked them with a stick to keep them moving. The boy spotted him and shrank back in a doorway as if afraid of being seen. Fargo approached and stared curiously at the contraption, trying to make out what it was. It looked like a millstone in the center, but there was no grain being ground.

As if in answer to his unspoken question, the boy darted forward and threw a handful of grain onto the broad stone, ducking as the spokes went past him. The oxen continued to go around and around. The boy glanced over at him and sprinkled more grain on the stone. Fargo had the distinct impression that the kid was doing that for his benefit, because the boy had no interest in the grain that was ground up.

"What's your name?" he asked the boy in Spanish. But the kid was frightened and returned to the doorway, looking out at him, his face wary. He would get no information from the boy. Fargo puzzled over the machine a little longer, then wandered off. There was a lot that was mysterious in Los Ricos.

At the edge of the mesa, running the entire circumference, was a low white wall of stone. Fargo looked over it and down to the desert floor, hundreds of feet below. It was a long fall down a sheer cliff. He kept his eyes open for any break in the cliff below, any way that a man could climb up to the top of the mesa without using the narrow path at the front. But the mesa was impregnable from all other sides. Los Ricos was in a perfect defensive position, the town itself a kind of mirage, a green flowering paradise high above the desert, midway between the dry hell of El Diablo far below and the cool blue sky above.

As he was nearing the entrance to the village, he spotted the count and Serena up ahead, standing in the middle of a wide street along with a group of soldiers and General Vito Ramirez—on foot this time. As he drew near, he saw that they were gathered around the scarecrow figure of Hagan Crowley in his ridiculous plaid jacket. He was standing still in some kind of trance, eyes closed, his forked stick pointing down at the ground. The count spotted him and glowered. Serena noticed him, too, but looked away quickly. Today she was wearing a leather skirt and a tight red blouse that clung to every curve of her tiny waist and her full, high, mounded breasts. Her waist-length hair was loosely caught back in a red ribbon. Once again, he was struck by her pointed face, her catlike physique.

"What is this man doing here?" Aznar asked the general. The count seemed irritated.

"I have hired Senor Fargo to help us transport our shipment to Sante Fe," General Ramirez said coolly.

"What?" Count Aznar exploded. "Do you think that is wise?"

"He is exactly the man for the job," the general said. "Let me be the judge of that." The count seemed to back down immediately.

"Well, Vito," Aznar said, "you are always right about your men. If you think this one can do the job for us, I'm sure you are right."

"Well, I don't trust him," Serena spat in his direction. Fargo smiled innocently back at her and she flounced away, infuriated. He knew her type, cold one moment, hot the next. But if he had the general's trust and the count's assent, that was all that mattered.

The general and the count turned their attention now to Hagan Crowley, who was swaying above the street, holding his stick in his hands. Everyone was silent, watching. Fargo had seen men divining for water before. The West was full of diviners promising to find water anywhere. But Los Ricos had all the water anybody needed. What were they hoping to find up here on this high chalk mesa? Fargo was immensely curious, but he didn't dare ask. Instead, he wandered away to take a look at the entrance gate and to check on the Ovaro in the stables.

The black-and-white pinto was glad to see him. He had brought a couple of carrots in his pocket that he'd found growing in a vegetable patch on the far side of town. The Ovaro nuzzled him, and Fargo filled the trough with feed and gave the horse fresh water. The horse had been well cared for by the general's men.

Fargo emerged and stood by the wall at the entrance to the village, at the top of the steep narrow path that led down to the desert land far below. He spotted several soldiers, one at the top of a rock, another standing guard near the natural archway, a third barely visible down below. It would be impossible for anyone to sneak up the path to the village. Even Akando, who could move like the shadows of night, would find it impossible to get in without being seen. Fargo swore under his breath and wished he could communicate with the Indian, let him know he was all right. Fargo hopped up onto the wall and looked out over the broken dry land far down below. Akando was out there somewhere. Maybe he was even watching him right now with his sharp hawk eyes.

It was blazing midday and Fargo suddenly realized he was hungry. He turned about and headed back to the cantina. He passed Hagan Crowley, who was kneeling in the street, putting his forked stick away into a leather satchel. Inside, Fargo could see other forked sticks. There was no one else in sight, except for an occasional soldier walking by, rifle on shoulder. Fargo waited until the skinny fellow stood up and then fell into step beside him. They were both heading toward the cantina to get something to eat.

"Any luck?" Fargo asked, nodding toward the bag Crowley carried.

Hagan Crowley glanced at him swiftly, his pale eyes darting in his flushed face. He shook his head, took off the straw hat, mopped his brow, and raked his fingers through his carrot hair. Fargo was hesitant to ask what it was exactly that he was looking for.

"I'll probably spot it this afternoon," Crowley said after a pause. He sounded nervous though. "Yeah," he added, as if to convince himself. "Definitely this afternoon."

Inside the cool darkness of the cantina, men were lined up at the bar, and the old bartender was dishing out bowls of chili. Piles of fresh tortillas were in plates on the tables. General Ramirez, Count Aznar, and his daughter sat at a table in the corner. Fargo went to join them. He sat down next to Serena, who refused to look in his direction.

Ignacia arrived with a tray of chili, hot tortillas, a plate of sliced beef, and fresh avocados and peaches. She glanced covertly at him, and Fargo could see the smile behind her eyes. That was the kind of woman he respected. No games.

She was bending over, serving the count some beef, when Aznar suddenly announced he was hot and stood up to take off his coat. Fargo tried not to look in their direction, but he heard Ignacia offer to help the count and he knew she was trying to steal the piece of paper out of his jacket. A moment later, he glanced up and caught sight of her tucking the paper into the pocket of her dress. She caught his gaze and nodded very slightly. Good, she had it. Without a backward glance, she deposited the tray on the bar and then went outside.

Fargo waited a few minutes and then left the table and followed her. He saw her motioning him from the doorway of the church. Few of the soldiers were around at this hour and no one seemed to be taking any notice of them. He quickly crossed the plaza and followed her inside.

In the dim light of the cool sanctuary, Ignacia pulled the slip of paper from her pocket and held it flat in the dim light. The words were printed by hand in Spanish:

I know a town, Los Ricos,
where nobody gets old.
I know a town, Los Ricos,
built on land of gold.

Beneath the streets of Los Ricos,
is the rarest golden honey.
Everyone's rich in Los Ricos,
but nobody has any money.

Oh, those rich men of Los Ricos,
everybody is blind.
The jewels of green, red, and yellow,
would be so easy to find.

Oh, those rich men of Los Ricos,
the village without greed.
If you find the secret of Los Ricos,
you'll have everything you need.

"But this is a song everybody knows!" Ignacia
muttered after she had read the first line or two.
When Fargo finished reading it, she hummed a
tune, then sang several of the lines. "No wonder it
sounded familiar last night. Everybody knows this
song about Los Ricos. This is no secret. It is not
important."

"But Count Aznar thinks it is," Fargo said.
"What does the song mean, anyway? It talks about
a land of gold, colored jewels, and some kind of secret of Los Ricos."

"Oh, it's just an old song," Ignacia said impatiently. "We are a poor town. It doesn't mean anything."

Fargo half believed her, but behind her words he
could also hear that she was holding something
back. There was some secret she was not telling
him. As if she could read his thoughts, she whirled
about and left the church. Fargo waited for a while
and then followed her. When he arrived back in
the cantina, the count and Serena had left. Only

the general remained. Ignacia was pouring him a glass of beer and he was looking up at her appreciatively. She ignored his gaze, but when Fargo met her eyes she shook her head very subtly. Obviously, she hadn't managed to get the paper with the song back into the count's pocket before he had left.

Fargo sat with the general for an hour, and the commander was in a talkative mood. Once he had decided that Fargo was a mercenary, all his defenses and his suspicions had dropped. He told Fargo several very long stories about his exploits throughout the territory, running down Apaches and bandidos, wreaking revenge on the troops of his political opponents. After a while, Fargo got the feeling that the general saw the world as full of enemies. Everyone, it seemed, was either the general's ally, or his opponent, and deserved to die— what a helluva way to live.

While he listened to the general, Fargo was thinking of Akando. How long would the Apache wait around out there? And how much of what was going on at Los Ricos would the Indian be able to guess at? If only there were some way to signal him and talk to Akando, let him know what was happening. All he could do was hope the Apache was keeping a sharp lookout on the mesa.

The general finally tired of talking, and the cantina was deserted. He rose from the table and straightened his uniform.

"It is the siesta," he said, "and time for the little sleep. You too, Senor Fargo?"

"I think I'll go check on my horse," Fargo said, as an excuse to get away.

"I saw that Ovaro in the stable," the general said. "I am the connoisseur of horses—very fine and very rare. Deep chest. So, you go and look at your horse; I am to sleep." The general walked up the stairs to find his room, and Fargo left the cantina.

Outside, the sun was blasting hot and reflected bright white on the buildings of Los Ricos. A few soldiers walked slowly down the street, but the village seemed sleepy. Fargo led the Ovaro out of the stable and then rode it through the village streets for a half hour to give it some exercise. It needed a good run, but at least this was something. Then he tethered it outside the stable, near some window boxes full of herbs and a gutter running with fresh clear water.

A short distance away, Fargo spotted a low wall shaded by two lemon trees, with cool water running nearby. He sat down in the shade, washed his face in the water, which tasted slightly sweet, and rested back, his hat brim pulled low. Between dozing, he kept an eye out, but all was peaceful in Los Ricos.

The sun was lowering and the shadows were just beginning to lengthen through the streets of Los Ricos. Fargo had just awakened and stretched himself. The pinto had happily munched almost the entire window box of greens and looked content. Fargo had just loosened the tether and was about to lead the pinto back into the stable when he heard gunfire and shouting from the next block. He left the Ovaro and sprinted in the direction of the sound, along with many of the soldiers heading in that direction.

As he rounded the corner he saw a group of soldiers gathering around something. Several of them were firing into the air with excitement. Fargo pushed through the crowd. At the center, he saw Hagan Crowley standing with his forked stick pointing straight downward. The stick was shaking in his hands, and Crowley had a wild look on his face, his pale eyes darting skyward. His shoulders were shaking as if he could not control the movement of the stick. Fargo had seen some divination before, but this guy really put on a show.

"Attention!" a voice called out in Spanish.

The men fell back immediately into straight rows. Through them hurried General Ramirez, followed by the tall count and Serena. They had all obviously just awakened from their siestas. The general caught sight of Crowley and stopped short.

"You have found it?" he asked. "After only one day?"

Crowley's eyes focused on the general and he winced, seeming to jerk on the forked stick, as though wrenching it away from some magnetic power. He took a stumbling step backward, then wiped his forehead.

"He's very fast," Serena said. "I told you, we saw

him find the Countess Allende's necklace in only one hour! It was amazing."

"This is the spot?" Count Aznar asked.

"Yep," Crowley said. "It's a damn powerful pull. One of the strongest I've ever felt. Got to be a lot of treasure down there. Heaps and heaps. I never felt anything so strong."

Several of the soldiers stole glances at the stone street. Treasures, Fargo thought to himself. That's what they were after. But he didn't believe for a moment that Hagan Crowley could find anything, much less buried treasure, with that stupid stick of his. Why the hell did they think it was buried here anyway?

"My men will begin the excavation immediately," the general said. He gave quick orders and several men ran off for equipment. "Just how far down is it?"

Hagan Crowley loosened his collar and nervously looked around.

"Well, General, that's just the problem with these sticks. I know it's down there, directly down there, but I just can't tell you how far underneath it's buried. These sticks won't tell me that. Might be six inches, might be thirty feet."

"Thirty feet!" the general said.

"Might be all the way in China," Fargo muttered under his breath. Serena overheard him and scowled.

"One time I found a vein of pure emeralds in the mountains of Peru," Crowley said. "Why, I was

88

working for the Duke of Devon and he only had to dig two inches before he struck 'em."

"The Duke of Devon?" Count Aznar asked. "Do you mean Lord Ramsay? Why, I must ask him about that. How extraordinary. Last time I spoke to him, he was complaining of having no money. Just how long ago was this?"

"Just last year," Crowley said, putting his forked stick into his leather bag. "Yeah, last year. But maybe I got the wrong duke, come to think of it. Maybe he said Sussex or someplace like that. I get all those lords mixed up."

Like hell he did, Fargo thought. A man would have to be a blind idiot not to see what was going on here. Hagan Crowley was a complete fraud. And a bunch of fools were going to spend the next days or weeks or months digging down through the mesa to find that treasure.

Just at that moment, some of the soldiers arrived with pickaxes and shovels. Everybody stepped back and one of them took a swing at the street, breaking up the white cobblestones which were hastily thrown aside. Within a few moments, they had reached the dry soil beneath the street and several soldiers were beginning to throw shovelfuls of earth over their shoulders. Everyone else stood around watching eagerly, as though expecting at any moment to hear the dull thud of a shovel hitting a box of treasure. In every one of their faces, Fargo could see the blindness of greed.

"Well," Hagan Crowley said, sidling up to the

count, who was watching the hole being dug, "I guess I'll be getting along. Just like we said, I'll take half my pay now. And here's my address. You can forward the rest to me when you hit the treasure."

The count nodded absentmindedly, his eyes never leaving the work. He pulled out his wallet and counted out a dozen large gold coins and put them in Crowley's palm. The figure in plaid moved slowly off down the street, lugging his big black bag. Some racket, Fargo thought. The charlatan would collect half his big fee and the fools would keep digging until they finally gave up. If they found him again, he could always say they didn't dig down far enough.

Ignacia came running down the street and obviously had heard the news. She pushed through the soldiers and came to stand near Fargo. In the hubbub, she spoke to him.

"I never got the paper back into the count's pocket," Ignacia whispered. "Do you think he'll get suspicious if he finds it's missing?"

"We can't afford that," Fargo said. "Give it to me and I'll try."

Ignacia pulled the small folded paper from her skirt pocket, secreting it in her palm, and passed it to Fargo. No one seemed to take notice of them. Fargo moved forward to stand next to Count Aznar. Serena was on the other side of her father. Now she was in one of her good moods, Fargo noticed. She smiled at him and he touched the brim of his hat. No need getting her riled up more than she was. One lock had escaped the red ribbon that bound her long hair, and it fell into the deep cleavage between her breasts, visible over the top of her barely buttoned red shirt. She played with the lock as her dark eyes held Fargo's. The count, standing between them, took no notice, but had eyes only for the excavation.

Just then, the men hit something. A sharp clink resounded against the metal of the shovel. A huge cheer went up and everyone pressed forward. Fargo took the chance, and holding the folded paper between his fingers, he lightly began to insert it into Count Aznar's jacket pocket.

An instant later, the count whirled toward him, grabbing his wrist. Fargo dropped the paper and it fluttered to the ground. Count Aznar's dark eyes were flashing and his silver hair gleamed in the sun. Serena darted forward and retrieved the paper. She stood and unfolded it, read it, and nodded to her father.

"So, you are the thief!" Count Aznar exclaimed. Several of the soldiers brought their rifles up at the sign of trouble. Meanwhile, over at the hole, the soldiers were getting excited, and he heard the ringing sounds of the shovels hitting something hard.

"I don't know what you're talking about," Fargo said.

"What's going on?" General Ramirez said, walking toward them.

"The prophecy," Aznar said. "About the treasure. I noticed this afternoon that someone had taken it from my pocket. Now it appears that Senor Fargo is the thief."

"I was curious," Fargo shrugged at the general. "Wanted to know what you were up to. Now I know. Buried treasure."

"Clever," the general said with an appreciative laugh. "It doesn't matter anyway. And you almost got away with it."

"I told you he was not trustworthy," Serena said.

Fargo tried to remove his arm from the count's strong grip, but he would not let go.

"So, when do we leave with the shipment?" Fargo asked the general, eager to defuse the situation.

"Shoot him," Count Aznar said.

"Now, cousin," the general said, "Senor Fargo will be very useful to us. It's one thing to dig up treasure. It's another thing to get it transported safely to the United States territories, where we can sell it for the best price and escape the imperial taxes of one hundred percent."

"I say shoot him," Count Aznar repeated, his voice cold. The general snapped his fingers, and two soldiers came forward and stood alongside Fargo.

"I agree," Serena put in. "We can never trust him. Who knows what he'll do next?"

The general considered for a long moment, distracted by the hubbub around the hole in the street. A groan of disappointment went up among the soldiers digging as one of them lifted a large stone out of the hole. Some treasure. General Vito Ramirez sighed with disappointment, stroked his three chins, and looked Fargo over, head to toe.

"Come on, General," Fargo said. "You'd have done the same thing in my position. The piece of paper's no big deal. You gonna kill me for being curious?"

"Please, Senor General," Ignacia said. The general turned to her with suspicion and she fell quiet.

"Yes, shoot him," General Vito Ramirez said.

4

Fargo tensed when he heard the general's orders to have him shot. Ignacia cried out in protest at the same moment that the two soldiers stepped forward to seize him. But Fargo was ready. With his powerful right, he swung out and slugged the first in the belly. The man's breath left him and he doubled over, while Fargo spun on one foot and kicked backward at the second soldier, catching him in the groin. The man went down. Fargo threw himself forward, knocking down Count Aznar and catching Serena around the waist with his left arm. He regained his balance, pulled her close, and in one smooth motion, drew his Colt and put the barrel to her temple. He jerked her around until he had his back against a wall. At the same moment, the soldiers all grabbed for their rifles and brought them up, aimed right at him.

"One move and she's dead," Fargo said, facing them down. None of them knew he'd never shoot a woman hostage, even if Serena wasn't exactly innocent. But this was a poker game now. And all that mattered were the cards he held in his hand and his ability to bet on them.

"Let her go, Senor Fargo," General Ramirez called out. "I have a hundred men here. You haven't got a chance."

"Even if you shoot me in the head, I'm gonna pull this trigger," Fargo warned. "And I got a hair-trigger finger." He kept talking as he slowly eased her away, inching along the wall. The soldiers kept their rifles trained on him. If he could just make it to the pathway that led out of town. The soldiers, the general, and Count Aznar seemed frozen. He could feel Serena panting with fear. It was important to keep talking to them. "You gonna kill me for being curious? You're gonna kill her, too. Seems like you folks aren't really to my liking as clients. Now, nobody move and nobody's going to get hurt. I'm just interested in getting out of here with my own skin. That's all."

"Then let her go," the general said.

"I'll let her go when I get to the bottom of the mesa. But one shot from anybody and she's dead. Got that?"

"Shoot him, goddamn it," Count Aznar hissed between clenched teeth. "He's bluffing."

"Shut up. What's our guarantee you'll let her go?" the general called out.

"I don't want you following me for the rest of my life," Fargo answered. "I'm not interested in a ransom. We'll just call this a business deal gone bad. You got your treasure and I'm out of here."

95

"Seems fair enough," General Ramirez said. "But if you don't let her go at the bottom of the mesa, we'll follow you to hell and back."

Yeah, well, they'd have to follow him to hell and back. Because the truth was, there was more to this than just his own skin. Fargo had heard the count and the general planning to kill everybody left in town. And he was beginning to understand why. If word got out that they'd dug up a treasure, the royalty in the capital would want their cut. One hundred percent might be enough. So, they had to keep it quiet. Real quiet. Until he could figure out a way to get the rest of the people of Los Ricos to safety, he'd keep Serena as a hostage.

"I'll let her go," Fargo said. "We got a deal?"

"Shoot him," the count hissed again, infuriated.

"Deal," the general said.

Fargo pursed his lips and whistled. The sound of hoofbeats came from a nearby street, and in an instant, the Ovaro appeared. He'd been damn lucky he'd taken it out of the stable that afternoon and then left it untethered. Now for the tricky part. If they mounted separately, the soldiers would have a clear shot at him. They'd have to walk down.

"Call your men off the guard posts!" he called out to the general. The general relayed the order, and in the late afternoon light, Fargo saw several men climb down from their perches and head up the path toward the town. He waited until they had all climbed past him and then they started down slowly, his feet feeling for each step, still

96

holding Serena. At his command, the Ovaro followed behind them.

"Don't try anything," he whispered into her ear. "If I stumble, you'll get a bullet in your brain." It was better to keep her frightened for the moment.

The path was as hard to descend as it had been to climb, the chalky rock unstable and the twists and turns treacherous. Over their heads rose the spectral white rocks and cliffs as the path led downward. Behind them, Fargo heard nothing but the creak of the saddle and the Ovaro's hooves slipping on the rocks. They had come to a particularly narrow pass, where the path lay all in shadow between two towering rock formations and they were momentarily out of sight of the top of the mesa where the general and the count stood watching.

Suddenly, he knew they were not alone. There was someone overhead. Fargo tensed and Serena felt it. She cried out just as a bullet zinged by them, missing Fargo's head by inches. Fargo shifted the aim of the Colt, bringing it up to fire back at the flutter of movement he spotted behind one of the high rocks. One of the general's soldiers trying to be a goddamn hero. Just then, Serena struggled hard in his grasp, clawing and scratching and biting his hand. At the same time, the dark figure popped out from behind the rock again and Fargo brought the Colt up to shoot, but the shot went wide as Serena knocked his arm. A second bullet grazed his right shoulder, biting deep into the flesh. The pain coursed down his arm, a river of fire and burning ice. Fargo cursed and fired again, but the ambusher had ducked.

Clearly word of the deal hadn't reached this soldier and he was trying to save the day. Hell, he had them pinned down. There wasn't a rock larger than a loaf of bread to hide behind here without retreating a hundred yards up the trail. Fargo's right shoulder was bleeding profusely, and along with the waves of pain, he felt a creeping numbness along his arm. Damn it. On the next shot, the soldier might get lucky.

"Let me go, you monster!" Serena spat at him, still struggling. She tried to bite his arm again, but he shifted his grip on her and she clawed at him. Drew blood, too, with her sharp nails. What a hellcat.

Fargo had had about all he could take. He spun the Colt on his index finger until he grasped the barrel, then coldcocked her. Not a light tap, either. Her knees buckled under her and her body went limp. She'd have a helluva headache when she woke. Fargo let her slump to the ground and waited, Colt at the ready, his lake-blue eyes cold and still, focused on the rocks above. He'd be damned if he'd hide behind some unconscious female. A moment later, the soldier stuck his head up and Fargo raised his arm to fire. In an instant, he knew something was wrong. The Colt wavered in the air and he could not get his hand to obey his command. Hell, the bullet wound in his shoulder was deeper than he thought. He dove sideways just as the bullet whined by, ricocheting off the rock.

A second shot came closer behind, but an instant later Fargo heard a cry. He rolled to his feet and glanced up, seeing two men struggling on the rocks above, one throttling the other. In a moment, the soldier sank to the ground and the second man came leaping from one rock to the next, descending toward them. It was Akando.

"Strange pueblo," Akando said, nodding toward the top of the mesa. His eyes took in the bloodied mass of Fargo's shoulder. Without another word, he picked up Serena's inert body, and the three of them hurried down the hill. It was a damn good thing Akando showed up, Fargo thought. His right arm hung uselessly at his side. It had gone all numb and the blood dripped from it down the trail.

When they emerged from the narrow pass and could see to the top of the mesa again, Fargo saw that the echo of the gunfire had caused a great deal of excitement. They were too far away to hear voices, and the figures were small as ants. But he could see the dark line of soldiers pouring down the trail in pursuit, figuring something had gone wrong. And he knew they could see him well enough to count three figures instead of two. Count Aznar and the general would be wondering what the hell was going on.

"I said I'd leave her at the bottom of the mesa,"

Fargo said to the Apache, "but we're taking her along."

They were moving fast now, at a hard run, skittering down the trail. Behind them, far above, Fargo could hear the faint pop of gunfire as the troops gave pursuit. The trail was still too precipitous for him to ride the Ovaro and make good time, but the horse followed along behind. In another quarter mile, the trail grew less steep. Akando made a clicking noise with his tongue and his Appaloosa appeared from behind a rock.

"Let's ride," Fargo said. Akando threw the unconscious Serena across his horse and mounted. Fargo did the same and they were off, Fargo in the lead. Their mounts were surefooted, taking the rest of the descent like a controlled fall, plummeting through space, then catching themselves on their powerful legs, their hooves skittering over the dry rock. In moments, they had reached the dry flat ground of the El Diablo. Fargo glanced back up at the imposing mesa and the wavering dark line of soldiers and horses moving down the winding path behind them. From the top, the lookouts could see for tens of miles in every direction. They would watch and see where Fargo and Akando went. So, where the hell would they go?

"Hills," Akando said, as if reading his thoughts. Far across the flat, speckled with dry mesquite, were low sere hills, washed golden by the lowering sun.

They sped across the alkali-washed land, their

horses raising a white dust plume behind them that rose high against the sunset. Speed was all that counted now, Fargo realized. They had two fast horses, and if they could just get to the hills and keep moving through nightfall, they could find a way to hide their trail. That would keep them safe for the moment.

The Ovaro was galloping hard under him, forceful legs driving its hooves that churned the earth. Fargo pulled up a little as the Appaloosa fell behind. The other horse was carrying Akando and Serena's weight as well. His right arm still hung useless, and it was throbbing painfully. Try as he might, he couldn't move it. The blood had stopped flowing, but it had caked on his sleeve. Hell, without his gun hand he was almost worthless. But there was nothing more to be done until they stopped and holed up somewhere. That might be a while.

The sun had gone down behind the hills to the west, and a rosy glow lit the sky. Fargo turned around in his saddle and looked behind them. They'd made a good fifteen miles already at a fast gallop. The Los Ricos mesa was melting into the other mesas that stood behind it. But at the base of it, Fargo could see the dust plume of their pursuers, a distant smudge across the vast flat land. General Vito Ramirez and Count Aznar were bound to be hopping mad that Fargo had made off with Serena, after all. And the general knew this terrain. He also knew that once Fargo reached the hills, it would be damned hard to track him in the middle of the night.

For the next hour, Fargo and Akando rode the horses hard as the light faded from the sky and the first stars appeared. The moon would not be up until well after midnight, which was just as well—they needed the long hours of darkness. Fargo had time to think about what to do next. For the moment, it was a standoff. Fargo had Serena, and the troop was, in essence, holding the town of Los Ricos hostage. But the general and the count didn't know that Ignacia—or any of the other townspeople—mattered to Fargo. They had no way of knowing that Fargo had really come to Los Ricos because a padre named Salvatore had asked him to. As far as they knew, Fargo was just in it for whatever money he could get.

For the moment, the townspeople were safe. The general and the count would be preoccupied trying to rescue Serena and, once they got her, excavating for the treasure. He'd bought some time. But what would his strategy be? As the hills came nearer and nearer in the dusk, Fargo thought over every possible angle. But every plan he could think of came down, at the end, to him and Akando fighting a trained army of a hundred rifles holed up in an impregnable stronghold with a limitless supply of water. The odds were bad. Real bad.

The hills seemed to open their arms in welcome as they galloped into the folded land. They pulled up the horses and cantered side by side, letting the mounts take a breather. Serena was still out cold, and Fargo hoped she'd stay that way for a few more hours.

"Rocks that way," Akando said, pointing to the southwest.

"You lead," Fargo agreed. He was always impressed by the Apache's ability to disappear into the landscape. Every time he and Akando rode together, he picked up a few new tricks.

Akando did not disappoint him this time. They rode in the dim starlight through hilly land tumbled with rocks that seemed like gigantic heads with weird expressions. Akando knew exactly where he was going, and soon they paused at the top of a dry barren hill, looking down at a wide valley. Sometime in ancient times, molten lava from a volcano had poured across this valley floor, covering the earth and hardening into strange curving formations. The rock, which stretched for a long way through the long valley, was surrounded by dry yellow grass. Akando dismounted, walked twice around his horse, pointedly leaving his footprints. Following Akando's lead, Fargo did the same. He was looking down at the dusty ground, visible in the starlight, when suddenly he stopped, spotting strange tracks. He knelt to examine them.

"Sidewinder," Fargo said, seeing the looping sinuous tracks of the deadly rattlesnake. He'd have to remember to shake his boots out in the mornings.

"They see us go onto the rock," Akando said as they mounted.

Fargo followed as they descended the small slope and the horses clattered up onto the slick solid rock. At Akando's signal they reined in and dismounted. Akando turned about, and leading the Appaloosa, carefully stepped back onto their tracks. He led his horse for a good twenty yards, then turned at a right angle, leading it into the deep yellow grass. Fargo smiled at the Apache's cunning as he followed with his Ovaro.

Oh, yes, it was perfect. The general would be tracking them and would reach the hill at about moonrise. The general would spot their tracks in the dry dust and would see the rock valley ahead. He would know that a long night and probably a full day of searching would lie ahead of him. He would order his troops to descend onto the lava field and fan out to examine the entire edge of the huge rock formation to find out in which direction Fargo and Akando had headed. And as the general and his troop eagerly galloped down the hill and climbed onto the rock, they would not be looking carefully at the ground. Their own tracks would obliterate the trail left by Fargo and Akando. It would be a day or two at the least before the general got the idea to search the grasslands in front of the lava rock. And it might never even occur to him. In any event, by then Skye and Akando would be far, far away, their trail cold and almost useless. Oh, yes, it was perfect.

They climbed the hill of grass until they were out of sight of the lava rock valley, then paused on a slope of scree and dismounted. Akando disappeared over the hill, and Fargo knew he was retracing their steps in his soft moccasins, working by hand to obliterate as much of their track through the yellow grass as possible. The Apache would tamp the earth, erasing hoofprints, and comb straight the broken blades of grass. While he waited, Fargo loosed the bandanna from his neck and tied it tight around his shoulder. He felt the wound gingerly and was surprised to feel the lump of the bullet lodged there. He had thought it was just a graze. For a moment, he considered cutting the bullet out right then, but realized they couldn't spare the time. Serena, thrown across Akando's horse, moaned and started to slip off. Fargo moved forward and caught her with his good arm, keeping her upright on her feet. For a moment he enjoyed the feel of her tiny waist in his arm.

Serena grimaced and her eyes fluttered open. She moved her hand to her head and rubbed it. Her hair had come loose and the ribbon hung entangled. For a moment, her face was a blank, and then she remembered what had happened. She started and looked about as if hoping to see something familiar. For a long moment she was silent, as if trying to figure out what to do.

"Where are we?" she asked. He saw a slight flicker of craftiness in her face, a subtle alertness like a cat planning to pounce.

"About a hundred fifty miles from Los Ricos," Fargo answered her as he stepped away. "I'm afraid the general lost our trail a good seventy miles back. They went the wrong direction. You've been asleep a whole day." It was a complete lie. They were only about thirty miles from the village, but he didn't want her getting any bright ideas about leaving bits of clothing as a trail for her rescuers. The ruse seemed to work. The slight hope left her face and he saw her despair.

"What are you going to do with me?" she asked, her voice bleak.

"I don't know yet," Fargo said honestly. "Maybe ransom you." He accidentally brushed against the side of the Ovaro and winced as his wounded shoulder exploded again in pain.

"You deserve that," Serena said. "I wish whoever shot you had better aim." Fargo remained silent. What a bitch. "So, I guess you're just after ransom money."

"No," Fargo answered. "Actually, I was thinking of a trade. I'll return you if they let all the people of Los Ricos come out safely."

"Those peasants!" Serena said. "What do you care about them? Old women and babies. There's hardly anybody left in that ghost town, anyway."

"Thanks to the general," Fargo said. "He's recruited all the men of Los Ricos by force. Only once they're in his army, they all seem to get themselves killed. Nobody ever comes back to Los Ricos. Why is that?"

"Because they're troublemakers," Serena snapped, her eyes flashing. "The men of Los Ricos are all part of that gang of bandidos. They all secretly work for Jorge Gomez. Vito knows that, so once he gets them in his troop, he finds a way for them to die doing their duty. Peasants, all of them. Ignorant and dirty. They are always causing him so much trouble. But now he's almost got them wiped out once and for all."

"By killing all the women and children and making it look like the Gomez gang did it? Just so he and your father can keep that treasure all for themselves? That's worth killing women and children?"

Serena was silent for a long moment and he could read the thoughts on her face. She was wondering how he'd found out all about their plan. And although he wouldn't call it remorse, he could see that he'd touched something in her.

A moment later, Akando appeared at the top of the hill. Serena, seeing his braided hair, bare chest, and buckskins, shrank against Fargo in fright. Akando ignored her and mounted his Appaloosa.

"Who is that?" she whispered, her voice quivering. Yes, she was really afraid of Indians. Fargo didn't bother to answer her question. He'd seen this kind of fear before. It was usually because people had only heard things about the Indians and had never met one up close.

"Get on," Fargo said. She mounted the Ovaro, and although Fargo was prepared for it, she did not try to ride off and escape. Good. He'd convinced her it was futile. Fargo mounted behind and wrapped his arms around her. The right shoulder was throbbing, beating in his brain and body like a big bass drum of pain.

Akando led off again, and as Fargo followed, he tried to concentrate on the softness of her rear pressed up against him on the saddle, the lemony smell of her neck. That kept his mind off the pain. So did the occasional view of her breasts, full and hard-nippled, that he could glimpse inside her shirt as he looked over her shoulder. Good distractions as they rode through the long night.

By daylight they were high in the hills. As the first light came, they were winding up a riverbed that was dry as dust. No water anywhere in El Diablo. Fargo was glad he'd filled his canteens on one of his visits to the Ovaro in the stable. They had enough to get by, on strict rationing, for about a week. But for now it was time to rest. The horses were tiring and his shoulder and arm had gone completely numb.

Fargo pointed to a rock outcropping ahead, at the point where the dry river forked, leading to two smaller canyons. From the rock formation, one had a good view of the valleys. Akando nodded and followed as Fargo guided the Ovaro upward, through the rocks, until he found a small clearing, sheltered on all sides. They left the horses here and took the saddlebags with them, climbing a few yards upward until they reached a shelf, like a smile in the rock, with a rock wall like a row of bottom teeth. It was dry and snug with a ledge and sandy floor. Here they would be hidden from view but could easily see anybody coming. And they needed a full day of rest now.

"You lie down over there," Fargo instructed Serena, tossing her a blanket and indicating a place far away from the entrance. She opened her mouth to protest, then caught sight of Akando's face and did as she was told. Fargo and Akando stacked their rifles and guns at the entrance of the overhang, as far from Serena as possible. All three of them took a swig of water. Akando left for a while and then returned with a handful of dried herbs, which he deposited in a pile nearby.

"Now?" Akando asked. He drew a long knife. Serena, watching, gasped, not knowing what was coming. Fargo nodded and knelt on the floor. Akando produced a canteen, and a thick twig which he handed to Fargo to bite down on if the pain got too bad. Akando untied the bandanna from Fargo's shoulder and, with a deft motion, sliced the shirt caked with dried blood from Fargo's shoulder and pulled it away. The wound opened up again and the smell of blood filled the small enclosure.

Serena huddled against the wall and watched in horror. For all her tough-girl act, Fargo thought, she was not all that brave. He concentrated on watching her reaction to keep his mind clear as he felt the hot blade bite into his shoulder. The bullet was lodged deep. Akando grunted a few times, concentrating on trying to pop the lead out of his flesh while cutting as little as possible. The pain came in waves, as it always did, Fargo thought. He concentrated on the shape of the pain, the rise of its intensity, the burning sensation along the nerves of his arm all the way into his fingertips, as if he'd stuck his arm in a roaring fire. He heard and felt the bullet grinding against the bone of his shoulder as Akando dug around it. The scene spun around him and he put the twig in his mouth and bit down hard until the whirling stopped. Akando stanched the blood with the rags of the shirt. Hell, he hoped the impact hadn't shattered the bone. He dismissed the thought from his mind and concentrated again on Serena Aznar.

She huddled against the wall. The morning light, filtering into the rock room, illuminated her face, with its wide temples and black almond eyes, her pointed chin and small red mouth. She was so transfixed by the operation that she didn't seem to even notice him watching her. Her face was a mixture of pity, horror, and empathy, emotions he'd never noticed in her before.

"Bone is good," Akando muttered. The Apache grunted and made a final exertion, pinching the ragged flesh until Fargo felt something give way and the bullet was forced out. The pain was even greater as Akando plucked it from the wound and dropped it on a nearby rock. His shoulder was screaming with agony, his ears roaring, the hot blood flowing. Fargo bit harder on the stick, silently cursing the heartless General Ramirez, the Iron Thumb. The pain was burning up and down his arm, into his neck, along his spine. Fargo concentrated on that for a long timeless time. Then he smelled something and realized his eyes were closed. He opened them to find that Akando had packed the wound with the herbs and tied it with strips of his shirt.

Fargo removed the twig from between his teeth—there were deep marks in it and his jaw was stiff. He lightly touched the bandaged wound with his left hand.

"Nice job. Thanks."

"Lie down," the Apache instructed, shaking out the blanket. Fargo didn't argue, but lay on his left side. Before he closed his eyes, he noticed that Serena was still staring at him from where she was huddled by the wall. He couldn't read her expression. Sleep came quickly.

Fargo woke when it was nearly dark. He was alone in the rock shelter. He rolled over and felt the stabbing pain in his shoulder, but even so, he could tell that the firm bandaging would help the flesh to begin to knit. The smell of wood smoke and roasting meat met his nostrils and he saw that Akando had lighted a fire in the protected rock clearing just outside the shelter. He rose and went outside. The sky was filled with the golden light of sunset. Serena sat pressed against a rock, her face streaked with dirt, her hair wild. When she spotted him, her face showed relief.

"Are you all right?" she asked.

Fargo heard an uncharacteristic note of concern in her voice, and for a moment he thought maybe Serena was changing. But then he saw her glance at Akando and he realized it was only that she was scared of the strange Apache.

Fargo walked over to the fire where Akando was turning some strips of meat on several spits. From the shape of it, he could see the meat was snake. There wasn't much else in El Diablo. Akando was roasting some slabs of cactus, too. And there was a tin pot of coffee boiling. The Apache had undoubtedly gone through Fargo's saddlebags to see what kind of supplies he had, but had wisely decided to save the supply of pemmican and hardtack as long as they could scrounge up something else.

"The squaw is trouble," Akando said in Athabascan. Fargo nodded agreement. Serena shot them an angry look. She couldn't understand the Apache's language, but it was clear what Akando had said.

"Good for shoulder," Akando said, handing Fargo a tin mug of herb tea. It smelled horrible. Fargo drank it down, then stretched, moving his fingers, then his hand and arm. The arm was working again, but was sore as hell. For the next few days, he'd have to shoot with his left.

"Any sign of General Ramirez?"

Akando shook his head and stirred the fire. Fargo could see the Apache's eyes smolder and knew it was because the general was infamous

112

among the Apaches as a bloodthirsty murderer, brutally butchering their women and children indiscriminately and at no provocation, wrecking their villages, driving away and stealing their livestock. Akando and every other Apache alive would do anything to get his hands on Ramirez. Well, with any luck they'd get that chance.

Akando began lifting the strips of snake meat and cactus off the fire. Fargo speared some of them on a twig and handed it to Serena, along with a cup of coffee. She took it with a shudder of disgust.

"What is this?"

"Just eat it," Fargo said.

They passed the meal in silence. Serena picked at the strips of snake, wrinkling her nose in disgust. Fargo sat considering their options.

They had a good hideout here. They could see anybody coming for miles around and yet they were completely out of sight. For the moment, there was nothing to be gained by moving on to another camp. The problem was, he needed a strategy. The ace up his sleeve was Serena. Count Aznar would want his daughter back, and he and General Ramirez were no doubt mad as hell that Fargo had got away with her. So, maybe he could send a message that he'd trade Serena for the townspeople of Los Ricos. The problem with that was that the count and the general wanted to keep their buried treasure a secret—if they ever found it, of course. The Mexican government would want its cut of the treasure, and they didn't want to pay up. Probably by now all the black-shawled women hiding behind their closed shutters in that village knew what was going on in the street. On the other hand, if it came to a choice between his daughter and the treasure . . . But how could he negotiate with them? Could they make a hostage exchange safely? And what about the people of Los Ricos? Down here in Mexico, there was no law to appeal to. There was only the might of General Vito Ramirez in this part of the country.

Fargo swore to himself, then realized he'd spoken out loud. Time had passed. He looked up to see that the fire had burned down to embers and the desert night had turned cold. Serena sat dozing against the fire-warmed stone. Akando was looking up at the stars. The Apache glanced at him, his chiseled face a question.

"We stay here tomorrow," Fargo said. It was pointless to move on until he'd decided where to go. General Ramirez and his men were out scouring the land for them. And wandering was sure to leave more tracks and increase the risk of running smack into them.

Akando rose and took his bow and quiver, disappearing down the dark path. Serena stirred, then opened her eyes.

"Where did he go?" she asked.

"Akando? Off hunting," Fargo said absentmindedly.

"He's a savage, isn't he?" Serena asked nervously.

"No more than you or I," Fargo said. "Apaches have their own laws. And most of them follow their laws."

"Apache?" Serena stared, dumbfounded. "But Apaches are bloodthirsty bastards. They kill you in your sleep. They're murderers and robbers. They'll stop at nothing, they—"

"I think you have Apaches mixed up with General Ramirez," Fargo snapped. Serena fell silent and looked into the fire, brooding over his words. After a while, Fargo realized he was tired again. The shoulder was throbbing. It was a helluva wound. He signaled Serena to reenter the rock shelter, and he went in after her, carefully positioning his gun far from her sleeping spot and spreading his blanket in front of the door. The small enclosure was dimly lit by the red glow of the dying coals of the campfire. Yes, he was dog-tired because of the wound, the exhaustion coming now in waves, along with the pain. He'd sleep deeply, he thought. He glanced at Serena, who was spreading out her blanket. He couldn't trust her.

"Lie down," he said roughly. Surprised, she did, and looked up at him with sudden fear. Then she smiled slowly and raked her fingers through her hair. She sat up on her elbows and gazed at him, waiting. Fargo pulled a short length of rope from the saddle kit sitting on the ledge and knelt down on her blanket near her feet.

"Oh, you like ropes," she said seductively. The bitch, he thought. After playing all those games with him, now she suddenly thought he'd succumbed to her charms. He smiled to himself and began to tie her ankles together. His right hand was working well enough to make a good tight knot.

"What are you doing?" Serena said.

"Closing up for the night. On your side."

"Don't you trust me?"

Fargo didn't see fit to answer her, and he let her question hang in the air as he tied her hands behind her back and then ran a length of rope the short distance to his blanket so he'd awaken if she moved in the night. Without another word, he lay down and let sleep overtake him. Just before he drifted off, he heard her sniffle and then begin to cry quietly in the darkness. Served her right.

All the next day, they holed up, giving the horses a good rest. Akando had discovered a muddy water hole a quarter-mile distant in the dry riverbed, and in the morning, they gave the horses a good long drink. Serena, after a mild protest, used the brown water to bathe. Fargo sat on the dry bank and watched her hike up her leather skirt to reveal slender and very shapely legs. She noticed him looking at her and she fluffed her long dark hair out over her shoulders and then bound it back again with the red ribbon.

"You know my father and General Ramirez are going to find us, don't you?" Serena said. She bent forward to splash water on her neck and gave him a good view of her full breasts through the gaping neckline of her red shirt. "And when they do, they'll hang the both of you."

"Maybe, maybe not," Fargo said. "It's a risk I'm willing to take."

"For what?" Serena said, stomping out of the muddy water hole to stand next to him. "I don't understand you. You could just let me go right now and head back to the States. But instead you're hanging around here trying to save a bunch of worthless peasants. You're a famous man, I hear. Lots of people would hire you for all kinds of jobs. And you're risking your life for them?" She was incredulous.

There was no way to explain it to her, Fargo realized. She just didn't get it. He shrugged and got up to fill the canteens.

It took all afternoon for Akando to work his Apache magic and obscure all the tracks they'd left around the water hole. Meanwhile, Fargo and Serena returned to the rocky aerie to tether the horses. The sun was blazing down, but he decided to scout out the area and had to bring her along, not trusting her to stay alone. First they climbed up the rocky hillside until Fargo could see in all directions.

Far to the north, he could see the low outlines of the mesas where Los Ricos lay. He doubted Serena would recognize the land formation, however, and he didn't want her to know how close they actually were. All around, the wrinkled hills were dotted with ruddy rocks baking in the noon sun. At first, he saw nothing moving in any direction. Serena, after looking around, sat down impatiently on a rock as he continued to gaze out at the landscape, his keen blue eyes missing nothing. A few miles to the east, two eagles were in the sky. The heat rose in waves. The sweat trickled down his face. Serena sighed impatiently.

Something glittered on the plains beyond the hills to the north. He looked just near it and not directly at it, a trick he had learned after long years in the wild. Yes, a few men on horseback were riding out there, the distant dust plume barely discernible against the tan color of the dry land. They were fifteen miles away. Probably part of the army troop. They had split up for the search. That made sense. But it also made moving around in this land more dangerous. Fargo shifted his gaze to the area some miles distant where the lava rock field was and where they had, hopefully, thrown Ramirez off the track. He looked for a long time, but saw nothing. They were probably down there still, he thought, hidden from his view by the hills. What Ramirez needed was an Apache scout, but of course his hatred of the Indians made that impossible. Lucky for them.

"What are you looking for?" Serena asked.

"Dinner," Fargo lied. "I guess we're going to end up with some more cactus tonight."

"I never knew you could eat cactus before last night," she said, falling into step with him as they descended the rocky slope.

"There's a lot you never know until you have to," Fargo said. "Seems to me you've led a pretty sheltered life, shut up with all that highfalutin royalty."

"I guess," Serena said. "How did you get to know so much about the desert? Have you been through El Diablo before? It seems like such an awful place."

Fargo started telling her the story of his last journey through this territory, years before. About a gang of bandidos he ran down. About a cattle baron who'd tried to get more than he was owed. Even about the woman he'd known and loved and lost to the harsh desert land. All the while, he gathered the flat discs of prickly pear cactus, carefully cutting them with the knife he kept in his ankle holster. Serena held her leather skirt with two hands to make a basket to carry them in.

"And that's the story," he finished up.

"But you gave away the money you earned to that poor family," she said, shaking her head in wonder.

"Sure," Fargo said lightly. "It seemed like the right thing to do. They had nothing. And I knew I could always get another job, earn another pocketful of cash."

"I don't think I've ever met anybody like you," Serena said wonderingly. As Fargo watched her face, he saw her eyes fill with tears. She could be

119

very beautiful when she was just being real, he thought.

"Let's get back," he said, turning away and heading back to their camp.

Serena was following him down the rocky trail, some distance behind. Then he heard her stop.

"I think it's shorter this way," she called out. Fargo turned back in time to see her disappear between two rocks.

"Just follow the goddamn path," he swore under his breath. He had just turned to climb back up and see where she had gone when he heard her piercing scream.

Fargo ran up the path, his boots slipping on the hot stones, until he reached the place she'd turned off. He slipped between the two rocks and saw her standing, frozen, in the middle of a shaded rock ledge. She held her skirt filled with the cactus, and her hands were trembling. He could see the bare skin of her legs exposed.

At her feet lay three sidewinders, which had been napping stretched out on the shady rock. Now they were disturbed and they coiled and uncoiled nervously, slithering over the stone. One had already reared up into strike position, its strange hooded eyes trained on her, beaded tail lifted high in the air, the dry hissing rattle sounding, its mouth wide open with dripping fangs.

5

Serena stood still in horror as she gazed down at the sidewinder rattler at her feet, its tail beating a nervous song of death. Her bare legs were exposed beneath her raised leather skirt and above her boots. Her hands were shaking, and Fargo saw she was about to drop the cactus. The sidewinder was tensing for the strike, and the other two were rearing up as well.

"Listen to me," Fargo said in a low voice. He moved his left hand slowly toward the butt of his Colt. Damned lucky he'd switched his holster around that morning. "When I say, let go your skirt and raise your hands above your head. Fast—in one movement. Got that?"

Serena nodded, biting her lip.

"Now!"

The cactus cascaded down the front of her as her leather skirt dropped and she pulled her hands fast over her head. At the first movement, the largest snake struck, a blur of movement through the air, but just as he'd hoped, the snake struck against her thick leather skirt, which its fangs

121

couldn't penetrate. At the same instant, Fargo drew, and as the snake fell back onto the rock, he plugged it with a single shot. A second shot hit the second in the middle and it writhed, broken and bleeding among the pieces of scattered cactus.

As soon as the first snake hit her, Serena screamed and took a step backward, stepping on the third snake, which hissed and beat the rock with its tail, then coiled up around her boot, its head disappearing beneath the hem of her skirt.

Fargo swore and moved forward, seized the snake's tail and yanked at it. The force of it pulled Serena off her feet and she went down hard on the rock as the snake came loose from around her booted ankle. Fargo swung it over his head as it tried to coil and bite him and brought it down hard, smashing the life out of it against the rock. He stepped on the other snake's head as it was still shuddering in its death throes.

Serena sat stunned, holding her hands in front of her. They were full of cactus prickles. The tears were streaming down her face and she was sobbing, inarticulate. Fargo grabbed her booted foot and threw back her skirt, examining one leg and then the other. He breathed a sigh of relief. He'd managed to get the snake off her in time. Damn lucky. Sidewinders were fatally poisonous, and even if you cut the wound and sucked the venom out immediately, the victim usually got real sick for a couple of days. If they survived.

Fargo helped Serena to her feet by lifting her up

underneath her arms. Her palms were full of prickles and she was so frightened she could hardly manage to pluck them from her skin. Fargo helped her get most of them out, then led her to a rock to sit for a while. He gathered up the three snakes and kicked the cactus bits into a pile.

"Fargo?" Serena said. He glanced over at her. She'd got the cactus spurs out of her hands and she stood up, her face tearstained and her dark wavy hair going every which way. Her dark eyes were pleading, honest. She'd never looked more beautiful to him. "Fargo?" she said again.

He crossed over to her and she came into his arms and he kissed her, deeply, feeling her welcome him into her mouth, tasting her lovely sweetness and the lemony citrus smell of her, mixed in with the musky odor of her sweat. He nuzzled her hair and she clung to him, pressing the warm curves of her round breasts, her soft belly, against the hard muscles of his body. He felt the sudden desire rise in him, the wanting of her. She felt it too.

"Please," she said. "Forgive me . . . I, I want you, Fargo."

There were no other words necessary between them. He'd wanted her, too—yes, his body had wanted her from the first time he had spotted her from a distance, with her slender figure, the round womanliness of her, even her fiery spirit. And now she wanted him, too, fully, honestly.

Her hands stroked the broad muscles of his

back as he felt his hips moving rhythmically against her, his rock-hard cock erect, eager, straining to be inside her. She felt that, too, and gazed up at him, her eyes tender. Her hand moved down his hip and across to touch him there, her touch like a bolt of lightning, stroking the hard bulge of him beneath his Levi's.

He unbuttoned his fly and she took off her shirt. He cupped her beautiful round breasts in his hands and bent to kiss first one and then the other as she slipped her hand around his rod and began stroking him. He straightened up and suddenly she knelt before him, taking him fully into her warm mouth, swallowing him, tonguing him in a way he'd never felt before, sucking, pulling, flicking, the delightful shudders of sensation trilling along all his nerves, electric, radiating out from his penis through his whole body.

She began a slow driving, in and out of her mouth, and he watched himself go in and out of her as her tongue and her mouth held him and pulled him, and he felt his balls heavy and ready and the base of him like liquid fire, like a volcano about to explode, the molten lava gathering under pressure as she sucked his huge rod, back and forth, until finally, he could stand it no more and he shuddered, drove himself deep into her warm, wet mouth, pushing as he shot into her, spewing, the explosion of release, of ecstasy, coming and coming, again, again. She held his hips until he slowed and then stopped.

Fargo felt his breathing slow. Goddamn, she was good. He pulled her to her feet and kissed her again, fondling her breasts, marveling at the way her nipples crinkled with pleasure when he touched them. After a few minutes, he felt himself harden again as he thought of the rest of her. She noticed and held him in her hand as he grew. He unbuttoned her skirt, pulling it off along with her pantaloons, until she stood before him, stark naked but for her boots, her dark triangle glistening with the wetness of her desire.

Fargo put her hands around his neck, then grabbed her around the rear and hoisted her up. She hooked her legs around behind him and he brought her down slowly, easing his cock into her tight wet slit, letting gravity bring her down, slowly, around him. Then he turned and backed her up against the rock ledge and began pumping into her, harder, deeper, his rod swelling, less sensitive this time. She was slick and hot, palpitating around him as he drove into her.

"Yes, yes, oh," Serena breathed.

He ground into her, feeling her swollen button as he plunged and he felt her tense up, ready, and then, just as he felt her give way, she cried out and he released, shooting again, less hot this time, but steady, pumping relief, again, again, like a sobbing fountain as she contracted around him like a mouth, sucking him dry.

He slowed, then stopped and kissed her gently

on the eyelids. She looked up at him, her face openly contented.

"Thank you, Skye," she said.

"We're on a first-name basis now?" he teased her. "That's the first time you've called me Skye."

"Is it?" Serena asked with a laugh. They pulled on their clothes again. Fargo loaded her leather skirt with the pieces of cactus. As they started to leave, he picked up the three snakes.

"What are you bringing those for?" she asked.

"Dinner," he said.

"I'd never eat rattlesnake in a million years," Serena said with a grimace.

"You did last night," he pointed out.

Serena's mouth fell open. A moment later, she laughed. They were still laughing when they arrived back at the camp.

Akando was standing near the ash pit of the campfire, gazing out at the valley. As soon as Fargo spotted him, he knew there was something afoot. He came to stand next to the Indian.

"What is it?" Serena asked. "I don't see anything."

Fargo and Akando were silent, their keen eyes trained on the dry land below. Yes, Fargo was thinking. The Apache was right. Someone was out there, approaching. There was nothing a man could see or hear or smell. But something, call it instinct, told him that someone was coming. Then he caught the faint trace of rising dust at the end of the long dry valley.

"One rider," Akando said, speaking Fargo's thoughts. A scout, maybe? Hell, it would have to be somebody really good to have found their tracks. And if somebody was tracking them, they'd have to catch him before he could return to Ramirez and divulge which direction they'd gone. Fargo fetched his Henry rifle.

"Stay here," he told Serena. "Do I have to tie you up?"

"No," she said. "No, I'll stay here. I promise."

He looked into her eyes and knew that she was telling the truth. They left her and started the descent down the path to take up a position a little closer to the dry riverbed where they could have a clear shot at whoever was coming after them. A few minutes later, they were perched in tall rocks, gazing down at the valley where the bare brown sand curved like an empty road. They didn't have long to wait.

In a few minutes, a single rider came into view, his horse moving at a slow walk. Fargo expected to see a soldier, but it was not. It took a moment for him to make out the outline of the strange figure in the plaid jacket. It was Hagan Crowley, the diviner.

"What the hell is he doing out here?" Fargo whispered, wondering aloud.

"Lost," Akando said. And as they watched him, they could see that was the case. Crowley reined in his mount and took off his ridiculous straw hat to mop his brow. He seemed to be trying to figure out which fork to take. Finally, he kicked the horse and it started again, moving slowly as Crowley headed toward the left-hand fork. They watched him pass by and waited until he was out of earshot.

Akando glanced over at Fargo with a look that asked plainer than words, "Should we take him?" Fargo nodded his head in the direction Crowley had gone, indicating they might follow him for a spell and see where he was heading.

They set off, ducking from rock cover to rock cover as they followed him up the winding valley. Crowley never looked around and had no idea they were there. He was guiding his horse down the middle of the sandy riverbed, leaving tracks that a blind man could follow. Crowley seemed so oblivious that Fargo marveled he had survived as long as he had in the wild western territories.

They had gone a mile or more when Fargo felt the hair stand up on the back of his neck. He glanced at his companion and saw that Akando had felt it too. Something wasn't right. They were not alone. Down below, Hagan Crowley was heedlessly proceeding, his horse walking steadily along on the sandy track.

They had just rounded a curve in the valley when suddenly Fargo spotted them. The slopes ahead were dotted with huge sandy-colored tumbled boulders. And there were dark shapes of men, the curve of a shoulder here, the dome of a hat there, the sharp point of a rifle barrel protruding from behind cover. Ambush.

Fargo and Akando shrank back behind cover and watched. It happened fast and without a shot being fired. It was smooth, orderly, practiced. As Crowley's horse approached a boulder sitting in the middle of the streambed, two men suddenly leaped out from behind it. One grabbed the reins of his mount and the other pulled him down before he had a chance to reach for his gun. In seconds, he was surrounded by other men, and horses appeared from upstream. They bustled him off, and the men hiding above in the rocks swarmed down and headed out at a run behind them. In minutes, it was all over, as if they had imagined the whole thing.

"Damn good," Fargo said admiringly.

"Gomez," Akando said.

Yeah, Fargo thought. The Apache was right. Not only was the old Gomez gang renowned for cutting out their victim's tongues, but they were well trained and disciplined. But until he and Akando had found those peasants dead out in El Diablo land, he hadn't heard of Gomez for years.

He remembered that when General Ramirez killed the people of Los Ricos, he was planning to make it look like the Gomez gang had done it. What the hell was going on with the Gomez gang anyway, Fargo wondered. He remembered how all the men of Los Ricos had been taken away by General Ramirez and had died mysteriously. And how those peasant boys, out in El Diablo, had ambushed Count Aznar thinking he was General Ramirez. None of these bandidos had been boys.

There were too many questions and Fargo knew he'd have to get closer to the gang to get them answered. But just now his thoughts turned to Serena. They had been gone more than an hour now. The midafternoon shadows were gathering in the folds between the hills and he suddenly felt worried about her. Akando seemed to share his concern, and wordlessly they retraced their steps, hurrying across the dry slopes, wary and listening.

As they came into sight of the rock outcropping where they had camped, Fargo knew something was wrong. Deeply wrong. He swore to himself. With a glance, he told Akando they'd go in separately and that the Apache should hang back in reserve.

Fargo sprinted forward, heading up the path toward their camp. He never made it. Suddenly, from all sides, rifle barrels appeared, held by men in dark dusty clothing, and he felt something behind him and started to turn about just as something hit him hard in the back of the head.

The world spun around and sparkled for an instant as he fought the blackness that rose like gathering waters. With every ounce of will, he held onto consciousness and felt himself being dragged down the path and lifted by many hands and thrown over the back of a horse. He forced his eyes to blink open for an instant as they started off so he could get his bearings, see where they were going. The ground was spinning, his head was splitting, and the bullet wound in his shoulder was sending shooting flames again. Yeah, they were heading up the right-hand streambed. Fargo knew that the same men who had ambushed Crowley had got him too.

His head was clearing now but he didn't want them to know he had regained consciousness. He kept his body limp and loose and slowly turned his head, blinking his eyes open. Behind the horse he was slung over came another, and on it was Serena's unconscious form. Several men walked alongside. He closed his eyes again, then let his head bounce until he'd turned it the other way and could see where they were going. With a wave of relief, he realized that the Apache was not in the group.

For half an hour, the line of horses wound its way along the path. Then the men led the horses up a steep stone path and through several shadowy archways. Finally, they came to a halt and Fargo felt rough hands grab him. There was no need to keep pretending. As they pulled him off, he stood on his feet and opened his eyes.

In an instant, he registered the scene. He was standing in a deep natural canyon with tall stone sides. Far above, the afternoon sky was an oval patch of clear blue. The sunlight didn't penetrate to the bottom of this stone well, but all around he could see that the walls were riddled with natural caves, carved long, long ago when water probably ran through here. The caves were filled with canvas bags of supplies, and a string of horses were tethered to one side. He had been brought to the secret hideout of the Gomez gang.

Several men stood near him, covering him with their rifles as he looked about. They were locals, every one of them. Some wore the wool serapes of herders, others loose black cotton shirts. Their clothing was ragged and dusty. They stared back at him just as intently. Instinctively, Fargo felt for his gun, but of course they had lifted the Colt off him. Several of the men had carried Serena from the back of the other horse and laid her down on the bare rock nearby.

Fargo's attention was drawn by movement. The gang whispered among themselves. He glanced to one side and saw a small boy darting from behind one man to take cover behind another.

Then he spotted the familiar figure of Hagan Crowley. The skinny fellow had been tied to a rock and was out cold. As Fargo looked at him, Crowley nodded his head and groaned but his eyes stayed shut.

One of the gang cocked his rifle menacingly. Two others moved forward and held him by the arms. They weren't nice about it, either.

"Where's Gomez?" Fargo asked, breaking the long silence.

A man all in black with a trim mustache stepped forward. His face was long and thin, the cheeks lined with hard living. His black hair was graying at the temples and he had the air of a man who had the weight of the world on his shoulders. Yet he carried himself as a natural born leader. But as Fargo looked him over, he found it hard to believe the man standing before him was capable of the cruel butchery of ripping tongues out of men, living and dead.

"I am Gomez," the man said.

Fargo paused a long moment, knowing that his first words would be important. And might make the difference between life and death. But just at that moment, Hagan Crowley came awake and cried out in fear, looking around. Gomez glanced at him.

"Where the hell am I?" Crowley shouted, struggling against the ropes that bound him to the rock. He spotted Fargo. "And what the hell are you doing here?"

"You know this man?" Gomez said to Fargo as he nodded toward Crowley.

"I've met him," Fargo said. "His name's Hagan Crowley. He finds things. Like water. He's pretty harmless."

"That is for me to decide," Gomez said, walking around Crowley and regarding him closely.

"Let me go," Crowley protested. "You want money, you, you bandits, you can take every last peso off me. Get it right out of my saddlebags over there. That's right, take every last bit. But you got no right to tie me up like this—and just tell me, who the hell are you, anyway?"

"It's the Gomez gang," Fargo snapped at him. Crowley blanched; the color left his florid face.

"G-g-gomez?" His mouth gaped like a fish for a minute and then he started in again in a different tone of voice. "Please don't cut out my t-t-t . . . I mean, I won't tell nobody nothing, honest. You can trust old Hagan Crowley. I can keep any kind of secret—there's no need to keep me from talking. I can keep my mouth shut, really I can—"

"Then shut up," Fargo snapped. Crowley fell silent and the two men holding his arms smirked.

"Gracias," Gomez said with a little bow. He walked over to Serena's inert form and knelt down beside her, regarding her closely. "Pretty. Very pretty." He signaled for some men to bring water and he splashed some over her face. In a moment, she sputtered and came to. Gomez helped her sit up. When she realized he was a stranger, she drew back her hand, shook her head, and looked around, confused, then spotted Fargo. Her eyes were wide with fright. Gomez helped her to her feet.

"And who might you be, senorita?" he asked. She opened her mouth to answer but Fargo interrupted. Every instinct in him told him that if Gomez knew she was related to General Ramirez, she'd be dead. The Iron Thumb had been hunting for the gang for years. No, the truth was too dangerous. Before she had a chance to speak, Fargo interrupted.

"Serena Allende," he put in. "From up across the Rio Grande in Texas. I'm taking her to visit her father down in—"

The blow came swiftly. At the first sound of his voice, Gomez had whirled around and stalked toward him, then struck him in the face. Fargo's head snapped to one side and he felt his lip split and the blood flowing. Serena cried out and one of the gang restrained her from rushing to him. The two men holding him jerked him upright.

"Idiot! Why do you lie to me?" Gomez spat at him, his dark eyes flashing and his hand on the carved silver butt of the long-barreled vaquero pistol stuck in his belt.

"To save her life," Fargo answered.

"That is better," Gomez said, relaxing. There was a gleam of respect in his eyes as he circled Fargo. "I know who she is anyway. She is Contessa Serena Aznar. Closely related to Vito Ramirez." Gomez spat at the name, as did a number of the gang members. "And I also know this man was traveling through El Diablo with the count. And so were you."

"You've got good eyes," Fargo said. He licked the blood from his lips.

"Very good eyes," Gomez said. He nodded toward the two men holding Fargo, signaling them to release him. Fargo wiped his bleeding mouth on his sleeve, then put his hands in his pockets and felt something hard in his fingers—the turquoise turtle he had pulled off the dead man's neck.

"I see many things," Gomez continued, his gaze never leaving Fargo's face. "I see a famous man who is coming through El Diablo, riding on his famous black-and-white horse. I see him riding with Count Aznar and his daughter. I see him disappear into the village on the mesa. Then I see him running down the hill with the contessa. And I want to know why."

So Gomez had recognized him.

"I see many things too," Fargo replied. "I see young boys killed trying to ambush Vito Ramirez. I see a town with plenty of water and no men. I see two other men—they look like innocent men—lying out in the desert with their tongues cut out." He pulled the turtle out of his pocket and dangled the pendant on its chain in front of the face of Gomez. "And I want to understand why."

Gomez stroked his chin thoughtfully as he looked at the turtle. Then he slowly reached inside his shirt and pulled out an identical pendant, hanging on a chain around his neck.

"They were my men," Gomez said.

"Their tongues were cut out," Fargo pointed out. At the mention of it, Crowley was tugging again on the ropes that held him.

"I have never cut the tongue from a man, dead or alive," Gomez said.

"Now *you* are lying to *me*," Fargo replied.

"Everybody knows the mark of Jorge Gomez and his gang."

"Ah," the man replied. "But Jorge has been dead for ten years. He was my brother. Yes, he was a bandido and he was cruel. But I am Juan. Juan Gomez." Fargo believed him and the whole thing suddenly fell into place. He wondered why he hadn't figured out the puzzle before.

"You are men from Los Ricos, aren't you?" Fargo asked. "You ran away and are in hiding to escape the forced conscription."

"Some of us," Gomez said. "Others of us joined the army until we found out in time that Ramirez wanted all the men from Los Ricos dead so he can take over the town; I do not know why exactly. But I know the count is in on this conspiracy, too."

"And what about the boys?" Fargo said. "A bunch of boys ambushed the count, thinking he was Ramirez. You sending boys out to do your dirty work?"

"That was a tragedy," Gomez said. "The boys have escaped from Los Ricos, too. Their mothers send them here to the hills to be safe from Ramirez." He spat again at the name. "Those boys did not follow my orders. They were supposed to be my eyes, only to watch and to see. But they tried to be heroes."

Fargo became aware that Serena was twisting her hands uncomfortably. Tears were running down her face as she listened to them talk. She was finally feeling guilt at being involved in the diabolical plans of her father and his cousin, the general. Gomez

137

glanced questioningly at her and registered surprise when he saw her remorse.

"Enough of this, Senor Skye Fargo," Gomez
said, suddenly impatient. "Why are you sticking
your gringo nose into this affair? Is the famous
Trailsman hired by the count to guard his daughter? Or maybe the general wants you to find some
bandidos for him? Eh?"

"He's trying to save the people of Los Ricos,"
Serena said with a catch in her throat. Gomez
whirled about and approached her, standing close
to her and shouting into her face.

"And just why would he do that, senorita?"

"I don't know," Serena said plaintively. She sud-
denly broke down and sobbed, "I can't explain it."
Gomez stood watching her for a long moment.
Then he gave rapid-fire orders.

"Tie her up," he snapped. "And keep an eye on
her. Senor Fargo, you come with me." Gomez led
the way toward the caves and Fargo followed.

As he passed by the men who were tying Serena's hands behind her, Fargo said, "Go easy on
her." Gomez, overhearing him, turned around and
smiled.

"You are a man of great compassion, Senor
Fargo," he said. Gomez gestured for Fargo to enter
the cave, which had tables and chairs inside and
looked like a rustic cantina. "Yes, compassion,"
Gomez continued as they sat down. The tin cups
and a bottle of tequila were put down on the table

before them. "We have much to talk about, you and me," Gomez said, filling his cup.

And talk they did, as the sky overhead grew dim and then dark and the stars came out and spun in the sky. And as the hours passed, Fargo told Gomez all about the treasure that was supposed to be buried under the streets of Los Ricos and how the soldiers were excavating it. And after many hours, Juan Gomez finally told him the secret of Los Ricos, a secret that no man of Los Ricos had ever divulged to an outsider. And when Fargo understood it, everything made sense. All the questions he had had were answered. And then he knew that, at last, they had a chance. It was a slim chance, and a lot would depend on luck. But at least it was something.

Well after midnight, as he and Juan Gomez hunched over the table and the rest of the men gathered around them, they began to formulate the plan to recapture the village of Los Ricos and defeat General Vito Ramirez once and for all.

6

Just before dawn the next morning, Fargo left the hideout for a while and rode up and down the streambed signaling to Akando. Finally, the Apache came down from where he had been hiding in the rocks overhead, and Fargo told him everything that had transpired. The Apache did not smile, but Fargo could see the delighted gleam in his eye. This wasn't his fight, and yet the Apache was eager to do anything he could to help defeat General Vito Ramirez. And Fargo knew that although the Apache would not join the gang in fighting, he would be there, watching.

Fargo reentered the hidden canyon. It was Gomez who decided Fargo should be the one to explain their plan to Hagan Crowley. The lanky fellow was brought to them as they sat having a midmorning breakfast. Gomez offered him a chair and asked him if he wanted coffee.

Crowley scowled at them, rubbing his sore wrists, which had been bound by ropes all night. The coffee was brought and set down.

"So, you've gone over to their side now?" Crowley whined at Fargo.

"You might say that," Fargo said. "And if you want to save your life, you will too. Now, we've got a job for you, Crowley." Fargo explained it all carefully to him. How he had the important job of returning to Los Ricos around nightfall and telling the count that he'd ridden away only to discover that he'd used the wrong stick looking for the gold and he in fact suspected the gold was somewhere at the foot of the tall mesa and they should go right down the next morning and start looking for it.

Meanwhile, Fargo told Crowley, the Gomez gang, all thirty of them, were going to return to the foot of the Los Ricos Mesa that evening under cover of darkness and camp around the back side, inside a large rock overhang. Fargo made sure Crowley knew the spot he was talking about. They'd be tired, Fargo was careful to put in, because the whole gang had stayed up all night getting ready for the attack and they'd need a good sleep. But they'd get up early in the morning and get themselves in position at the base of the cliff and they'd ambush the general's whole troop once they came down the path.

"Right," Hagan Crowley said, nodding his head slowly. Fargo could see Crowley's thoughts written all over his face, the planned double cross. "Right," he said again. "So, I bring all the soldiers down with me at dawn to where you're waiting for them."

"Yeah," Fargo said, "but don't get there any earlier, or we won't be in position. And we'll be sure not to shoot at you, Crowley," Fargo assured him. "And when this is all through, we'll find that treasure you're looking for, and you can even have a big piece of it."

Crowley's eyes went wide and he nodded. "Got it," he muttered. "Bring them all down at dawn. Right."

Gomez sent him away and sipped on his coffee until Crowley was out of earshot.

"Will it work?" he asked Fargo.

"Oh, yeah," Fargo assured him. "Crowley's going to double-cross us, sure as I'm sitting here."

Moonrise was still a good two hours away by the time they were approaching the bottom of the mesa. They'd ridden to within a few miles of the tall rock and then dismounted, taking the rest on foot, hunched down, running swiftly across the dark land as they approached the gigantic rock.

Crowley had gone several hours ahead of them, on horseback, approaching in full view. Meanwhile, back at the hidden canyon, Gomez had left the boys with the job of watching over Serena.

They were running steadily toward the mesa, and Fargo wondered what was going on high above them in the village of Los Ricos at that very moment. He could just imagine it. Hagan Crowley would be spilling the whole story of how Fargo had kidnapped Serena and was planning the ambush. The count would be overjoyed that his daughter could be rescued.

And Crowley would tell them how the gang was going to be spending the night holed up in the shallow rock overhang around the backside of the mesa. General Ramirez would lick his lips at that, thinking of the desperate Gomez gang, along with Skye Fargo, trapped like mice in a hole, surrounded by his hundred troops who could slaughter them while they slept. And he would figure that his attack should come right in the middle of the night, along about two o'clock, just when the gang would be sound asleep. And Fargo imagined even now the count and the general were standing high above, watching the dim moving shapes approaching the mesa, congratulating themselves on their coming victory.

The base of the mesa, faintly luminous in the starlight, loomed before them. As they reached it, they proceeded around to the back side of it as they had told Hagan Crowley they would.

Gomez and Fargo were walking side by side as they approached the rock ledge. Gomez led the way inside and walked to one end. The men began removing several large rocks, the size of sheep, from the wall, and as Fargo watched, a dark opening was revealed.

This, he knew, was the secret of Los Ricos—the hidden entrance to the mesa town that every inhabitant was sworn never to reveal to any outsider. The very existence of the town depended on keeping the secret. Once the entrance was wide enough, Gomez crawled inside and Fargo followed him. Behind came the rest of the gang, leaving only one man at the entrance to give an alarm in case anything should go awry.

Juan Gomez struck a match, and Fargo found himself in a large room that looked like a natural cave in the rock. The men took up the wooden torches that had been leaning against the wall and lit them. Fargo spotted a wooden ladder resting against one of the walls. Gomez led the way, climbing up the ladder, and Fargo followed. When they came to the top, there was a small chamber, scarcely big enough for two men to stand in. Another ladder led upward, lit by the flickering torches.

For the next two hours, they climbed through natural caves and through some tunnels that had been widened by the inhabitants of Los Ricos. Sometimes they were climbing ladders and other times they squeezed between narrow rock passages or climbed on all fours across slippery rocks, helped by knotted ropes that had been left there for that purpose. From time to time, Fargo heard the sound of running water in the far distance, echoing through the cavern. Fargo marveled at the construction of the secret entrance to the village and asked Gomez about it.

"As long as we can remember, the people of Los

Ricos have had this secret," Gomez told him. "Many of the tunnels and rooms are natural caverns. But some of them had to be built to connect them all. When I was a small boy, I had the job, along with other boys, to come down and help the men widen the tunnels and keep the ladders in good repair. Also, to work on the water pump."

"The what?" Fargo asked.

"You think maybe the water at the top of the mesa flows all the way up inside this rock naturally?" Gomez laughed. Fargo paused for a moment on the ladder as the ridiculousness of the idea struck him. He hadn't thought of it, actually. But of course it didn't make sense. Water ran downhill. You couldn't have a spring gushing out the top of a mesa.

"The oxen," Fargo said with astonishment. "So that's why you have those oxen walking around in that circle continuously." Of course, the oxen pumped the water up from far below. And that also explained why the boy who was watching over them was scattering the grain under the stone. Because it was important that no stranger get suspicious and too curious. Anyone who found out about the water pump would also eventually figure out that there was a secret cave underneath.

"You understand that if an enemy ever knew how we get our water supply," Gomez said, "it would be simple to cut it off and that would be the end of Los Ricos."

Yes, it was an amazing secret, Fargo thought. He

remembered the song lyrics that Ignacia had stolen from Count Aznar's pocket. As they continued climbing, Fargo asked Gomez if he knew the song and told him about it.

Gomez laughed when he heard how the song had been interpreted.

"That's such an old song," he said, still chuckling. "I used to sing it all the time when I was little. My mother told me what it meant. The golden honey is the sweet water we have. And the jewels are the fruits on the trees, green and gold and red. The secret of Los Ricos is of course this cavern. And as for everybody being blind, it is because they pretend not to know the secret. You see, the whole joke of Los Ricos is the name. It means 'the rich ones.' But do you see any money in Los Ricos? No! But, you see, we are rich because we have water and food and sun, and that is everything we need."

Juan Gomez kept laughing to himself for a long time afterward, clearly amused by the idea that the general and the count would mistake a mere folk song for some kind of treasure clue.

They climbed higher and higher. Here and there, other natural caverns, dark and forbidding, branched off. As time went by, the sound of the rushing water grew fainter behind him, but now he caught the slight sound of machinery, of the creak of wood, the sound of the contraption that lifted the water up from the natural spring down below in the desert floor.

Fargo had lost count of how many ladders they had climbed and how many chambers and tunnels he had crawled through in their slow progress up through the very heart of the mesa. Fargo had the sense that they were nearly to the top when he, climbing a ladder, emerged through the floor of a large cavern. On one side he saw a huge wooden pole that was rotating, creaking slowly, as a seemingly endless row of buckets ascended, positioned on a kind of cable that passed over a wheel, up-ending them and dumping the water into a large pool. The emptied buckets then descended again through a hole in the floor. Gomez called a halt and all the men checked their guns.

Fargo had positioned the Colt to his left. His right hand and arm were still slow, stiff from the healing wound in his shoulder. Shooting with his left slowed him down, but only a little. But with any luck, they wouldn't be doing too much shooting.

That had been one of the tricky parts of the plan, Fargo thought as he followed Gomez up the ladder and watched the gang leader unlatch the wooden trapdoor in the ceiling. The hardest part of this plan had been figuring out how to even out the odds of thirty men against a hundred. Fargo had pointed out that even if they did manage to sneak into Los Ricos undetected in the middle of the night, a house-to-house shoot-out with the general's troops would be costly in lives, both in the gang and of the women and children left in the town. It had taken

Gomez a while to agree to Fargo's idea of how to defeat the general's men, but in the end he saw the wisdom of it and agreed.

Gomez had the trapdoor open now and was climbing through it. Fargo followed and stood up inside a storeroom. As the other men came up behind him, he moved to the window and flicked open the shutter. Outside, he could see the oxen walking around and around. The street was deserted. Fargo cracked open the door and a puff of cool night air wafted in. It was hot in the crowded storeroom.

They waited quietly, scarcely breathing, listening to the night. And twenty minutes later they heard it—the tramp of marching feet, the clank of rifles, the crackle of boots on the sandy cobblestones, low voices, the snap of issued orders.

This was it! General Vito Ramirez was getting his troops massed to sneak up on the gang at the foot of the mesa and slaughter them in their sleep. They waited until the sounds had died away in the distance and then they moved out. Fargo led the way. He eased open the door and slipped out into the street.

Hunched low, he sped along the side of the wall, keeping in the shadows. At the first corner of a building, he paused and peered around. There was no one in sight. He dashed across the open plaza to the cover of another shadowed wall. One by one, Gomez and his gang followed as they made their way, street by street, block by block, toward the main entrance of Los Ricos.

All had gone well until Fargo was crossing an empty piazza. Suddenly, a man in uniform appeared from around a corner and spotted him.

"Hey! You there!"

Fargo stopped, knowing if he ran he would blow the whole plan. The man was hurrying toward him, and Fargo could see the officer's epaulets on his shoulders. Suddenly, he had an idea and he snapped to attention and saluted.

It worked.

"Why are you out of uniform, soldier?" the man asked.

"General's orders," Fargo mumbled. "I'm in disguise."

For a moment, the officer believed him and came nearer.

"I didn't hear anything about—"

He never finished his sentence. Fargo dragged the unconscious man behind a low wall. Then he had an idea. While Gomez and the others kept watch, Fargo quickly doffed his hat and stripped off his clothes, putting on the man's uniform and pulling the duck-billed officer's hat low over his eyes.

They continued toward the main gate. Fargo walked out in front in full view dressed in the officer's uniform, while the others, hidden in shadows, followed. They were just a block away when Fargo heard the tramp of boots approaching. They couldn't have been in a worse position, in the middle of a block, too far from a cross street to get away. In an instant, the rest of the men took cover on either side of the street, ducking behind potted trees that scarcely hid them. Gomez knelt down behind a stone trough into which the sparkling water of Los Ricos was running.

Fargo retraced his steps and then reversed himself just before the small detachment of four men, marching in step, came into view at the other end of the street. The soldiers spotted him and saluted as they came nearer. They were so busy concentrating on him that they never even saw the dark waiting shadows on either side of the street. Fargo timed his approach carefully as the four soldiers came closer to where the gang was hunkered down.

"Halt," Fargo said in Spanish.

The four stopped, and just then one of the soldiers spotted one of the gang.

"Hey, who's that—?" But just then the gang struck, leaping out like cougars. The soldier brought his rifle up, but didn't have time to aim it. But he did pull the trigger. The sound of the shot resounded through the empty streets.

Fargo cursed to himself, hearing men shouting a block away and the sound of running feet.

"Get their uniforms," Fargo whispered to Gomez as he grabbed up the soldier's rifle. The gang lugged the four inert bodies away, running down the street. It was damned close. They had no sooner disappeared when three soldiers appeared at the other end of the street at a dead run. Fargo stood in the middle of the street and pretended to be examining the barrel of the rifle.

The soldiers came close before they saw Fargo's epaulets, and then they pulled up and saluted.

"Misfire," Fargo said in Spanish. "Get back to your posts."

The soldiers turned and marched off, but one was sufficiently suspicious to turn around and give Fargo a good long stare.

Fargo pulled at the tight-fitting military jacket and shouldered the rifle. Gomez emerged in a uniform and marched toward him, followed by three other men in uniforms. They marched in the direction of the gate, followed silently and stealthily by the rest of the gang.

When they came into sight of the main gate, Fargo saw immediately that they'd misjudged the timing a little. They were early. He waved the rest of the men back to cover in the street behind them while he and Gomez peered around the corner. The open area in front of the main gate was crowded with men scurrying around, fitting their bayonets to rifles, hopping into their tall black boots, and checking their ammunition. As they watched, the moon slowly rose and poured its silver light over the scene. The light gleamed on rifles and bandoliers filled with bullets. Beyond the gate, the light illuminated the edges of the crumbling white rock formations that hung over the path down to the desert floor.

As they watched, General Vito Ramirez marched into view, all five feet of him. Fargo could feel Juan Gomez, who was beside him, tense up at the sight of his enemy, his rifle trembling in his hand. Fargo put a hand on his arm to restrain him and Gomez nodded when he got himself under control again. The general called for his footstool and mounted his oversized bay.

Before him, the troops stood at attention in perfect formation. Fargo spotted Count Aznar and his big hired thug, Manrique, standing beside the gate to see the troops off.

Beside them was Hagan Crowley, and even from this distance, Fargo could hear Crowley's irritating voice boasting how, without him, the whole scheme would have been lost and the count would never have found his daughter again and on and on. Clearly, Crowley thought he was having the most successful night of his life.

General Vito Ramirez walked his bay back and forth in front of his men, looking them over. Then he drew himself up importantly.

"All right, men," he said. "You all know the plan. We march down. Quiet is the word. That renegade band is around the back side of this mesa, in a shallow rock depression. When we reach it, we will kneel in combat formation."

The general raised his short arm into the air dramatically.

"When I give the signal," he lowered his arm, "you will fire and reload and fire at will. I don't want anything larger than a spider to walk out of that cave alive. Are my orders clear?"

The troop stood at perfect attention. No one moved.

"Fine," the general said.

"Vito!" Count Aznar called out, anxiously.

"Oh, yes," the general said. "Following our victory over the Gomez gang, the first company will ride out with me to free Serena Aznar. Hagan Crowley will be leading us to the gang's hideout."

"Mr. Crowley, would you care to come watch the victory?"

Crowley hesitated only a moment, then agreed. A horse was brought forward for him and he mounted. The general nodded to his lieutenant.

"Attention! Right face! Forward! March!"

General Vito Ramirez rode his big bay toward the gate and disappeared down the path, followed by Hagan Crowley and then the soldiers. Fargo watched them go with a feeling of relief. So far, so good. In a few minutes, they were all gone. Other than Count Aznar and Manrique, there were six soldiers standing watch by the main gate of Los Ricos.

Fargo signaled for the three other men in uniforms to come forward to join him and Gomez. They formed a unit of five and marched forward. The rest of the gang held back, waiting in the shadows. The other three men approached the two standing guard, while Fargo and Gomez took up positions beside Manrique and Count Aznar.

The count was rubbing his hands in glee as he watched his cousin lead the troop down the winding path.

"Isn't it a marvelous night!" he said in Spanish, glancing at Fargo and then focusing his gaze again on the departing army.

Manrique grunted.

"Marvelous," Fargo said, repeating the word in English. The count froze in shock, then very slowly his eyes traveled back to Fargo's face. Fargo turned his head so that the moonlight fell across his features.

Count Aznar gasped, but his next move was instantaneous. In a flash, he pulled a small derringer from his pocket and fired, but the shot went wide because Fargo had already barreled forward and hit him. Gomez shouted orders for his gang to come out from cover just as Manrique made a grab for him.

As the Gomez gang swarmed forward toward the low wall at the edge of the mesa, the count fired again. This time, Fargo heard Gomez cry out and knew he'd been hit. Fargo wrested the derringer out of the count's hand and knocked him back against the stone wall just as he felt Manrique hit him from behind. Fargo whirled about to find that Gomez had gone down. He must have been shot bad.

Manrique, built like a grizzly bear, brought up

his pistol, but Fargo tossed the derringer into his left hand and fired, knocking Manrique's gun out of his grasp. Fargo pulled the derringer's trigger but it had jammed. He threw it down and pulled his Colt up just as Manrique hit him full force. They went down hard and rolled over in the street. Fargo lost his grip on his Colt and it spun away from him.

Manrique pummeled Fargo with fists of iron, and Fargo felt the wound in his shoulder open up again as pain exploded through him. In a black wave of rage, Fargo summoned all his strength. With a cry of fury, he suddenly thrust upward with his deadly left, catching Manrique under the chin and snapping his head straight back. The big man shook his head, dazed, then took a faltering step forward. Suddenly, Manrique threw himself down onto the street and Fargo saw him reach for the Colt and his big hand close around it. Manrique brought it up and fired just as Fargo leaped sideways. The bullet tore through the air.

"Shoot the bastard," Fargo heard the count mutter. All around him, Fargo could hear men shouting. The voices of the general's troops came filtering up from the distance, along with the occasional pop of a gun. Just then, the gang opened up with all their weapons, and the roar of gunfire filled the air.

Manrique hit him again, firing with the Colt. Fargo brought his arm up and managed to jostle Manrique's arm before his finger squeezed the trigger. The explosion of the gun was deafening. With a maddened roar, Manrique closed in once again, but this time Fargo was ready. He went down easily, letting his knees buckle under him. Manrique flew over him just as Fargo's hand found Manrique's pistol, and he rolled over on his back, bringing it up and plugging the big man. Once. Twice. It was enough. Manrique slumped down beside the wall and did not move again. Gomez also lay still. Fargo looked around for Count Aznar.

He caught sight of the count running away along the mesa rim wall.

"Halt or I'll shoot!" Fargo shouted after him. The count hesitated and Fargo gave chase. The count, seeing him coming, rifle at the ready, knew he didn't have a hope in hell. With one glance at Fargo, he climbed to the top of the wall, and looking out over the silent desert land of El Diablo, Count Aznar leaped out into space.

Fargo watched the dark figure, like a toy doll, falling and falling down the long cliff, until finally it came to rest far below on the rocks. Fargo glanced over at the gate and saw the gang lined up as they'd planned. But suddenly he realized that their plan might fail.

He raced back to join them. A quick look over the edge of the wall showed him that, once the firing began, the general's troops had taken any available cover. And now they were pinned down on the trail.

The Gomez gang was holding them there, popping up from behind the low wall to fire down at the hapless troop. But the soldiers could remain pinned down for hours, even days. And the longer they were, the more likely it was that some of them could escape, slipping away down the slope.

Another glance told Fargo that the general and Hagan Crowley, both on horseback, were already out of firing range, galloping hell-bent down toward the desert floor, followed by fully a quarter of the troop. He'd be damned if he'd let them get away. It was time for the last part of the plan.

Just then, Fargo heard a scraping noise behind him and he turned to see Juan Gomez dragging himself along the wall toward them. In the moonlight, Fargo could see that Gomez was badly wounded, the bloodied front of the uniform riddled with several bullet holes. But more than that, Fargo saw in Gomez's face the drawn and ghostly look of a man in his last moments of life. The Gomez gang stopped firing for a moment as they watched the man who had led them for the past decade in the lonely fight to try to regain the village that was theirs.

"Give the order," Fargo said to Gomez. "Otherwise, they're going to get away."

Summoning his strength, Gomez raised his hand in the air and brought it down. The Gomez gang raised their rifles and began firing again, but now they were aiming at the chalky rock formations high above the narrow path. Fargo helped Gomez prop himself against the wall so he could peer over. The gang fired again and again at the white cliffs. Nothing was happening.

"He's getting away," Gomez muttered in despair. And when Fargo looked, he saw it was true. In the stark moonlight, far below, Fargo could make out the figures of two men on horseback, Crowley and General Ramirez. They had reached the bottom of the cliff.

Just then, a resounding crack split the air, a sound like thunder. Fargo watched as the front face of the highest chalk cliff suddenly slipped, like a mask falling, and then tumbled into an avalanche, a rumble and a roar that filled the air, gathering more rocks and boulders that bounced down the slope, followed by tons of broken rock and soil, piling ton on ton, sliding down the slope, filling in the narrow path, burying dozens of men who screamed out in sudden realization, who tried to run in a frenzy, in a panic, caught by the sliding rocks, knocked down by the flying rocks and then buried forever deep in the mesa's white and stony mass.

A huge cloud of white dust rose into the air, obliterating the stars and hiding everything from view. The Gomez gang began to cheer their victory. Fargo and Gomez remained silent, staring out into the white cloud that hid everything below. The other men noticed their silence and fell quiet, then began slowly moving about, dragging away the bodies of the dead soldiers, stacking the rifles against a wall. It was a good ten minutes before the dust had cleared, and the whole time, Fargo and Gomez remained where they were, waiting.

Finally, the wind came up and blew the last of the dust cloud away. The Gomez gang hurried forward and stared down at the new tumbled slope which had completely obliterated the ancient pathway up to Los Ricos. It would never be as easily defended as the old narrow trail between the tall rocks, some of the men said, but it could be rebuilt.

But Fargo and Gomez did not look down at the path below. Their eyes were focused on the distance. There, galloping away across the moonlit plain, were two men on horseback.

Gomez swore and clenched his fists, his breath coming now in short gasps. Just then, another dark shape suddenly appeared, angling across the flat expanse.

"What? Who?"

"A friend of mine," Fargo said. "An Apache named Akando. He's got an old grudge against the general." They watched as the third shape suddenly merged with one of the escaping horsemen. The other horse ran on. Crowley was going to get away, Fargo knew. And that didn't really matter.

What counted was what he knew was happening out there, several miles from the tall mesa of Los Ricos. There, under the dispassionate stars, justice was being done. Akando was about to kill General Vito Ramirez. And before he let him die, he would take his scalp. And maybe his tongue, too.

Gomez was panting heavily now, trying to stand erect. Fargo put his arms around the man and helped him upright. Meanwhile, the men had gone door to door, waking up all the women and children who had remained in Los Ricos and were hiding in their houses. There were cries of joy and weeping, laughter and tears. Some men and women were dancing in the streets as the men, absent for years from their village, had finally returned to reclaim it for their own.

Gomez tried to speak, but his voice rasped. Fargo held up his hand and called for quiet. The villagers quickly fell silent.

"For many years," Gomez said, the words coming slowly, "I led you in exile. Now we are home." He paused for a long time. "You are no longer the Gomez gang. From this moment forward, you are only the men of Los Ricos."

The men cheered Juan Gomez. Fargo, his arm around the dying man, held him upright. As they cheered him, Juan Gomez died, his body suddenly limp, his eyes blank. Fargo let him down slowly and closed his eyelids. The cheering stopped and several men came forward to carry his body away.

Fargo turned to gaze out again at the quiet of El Diablo, thinking of Akando riding away back to his homeland with the general's fresh wet scalp. Count Aznar's broken body lay at the base of the cliff. And his daughter, Serena. What would happen to her? Come morning, he would ride back to the hidden canyon and bring the boys back to Los

Ricos where they belonged. And as for Serena, she'd probably head back to Spain. But he was sure she'd never be able to return to the life she had before.

He felt a hand on his arm and looked down to see the smiling face of Ignacia.

"Thank you," she said. "Are you ready to celebrate now?"

"*Sí, sí,*" he replied. He put his arm around her and they walked slowly toward the cantina, through the white streets of Los Ricos that glittered in the moonlight.

LOOKING FORWARD!
**The following is the opening
section from the next novel in the exciting
Trailsman series from Signet:**

**THE TRAILSMAN #176
CURSE OF THE GRIZZLY**

*1860, northwest Colorado—
in the shadow of Pagoda Peak,
where a dark prophecy is played
out to its terrible finish . . .*

Trouble.
Danger.
Signals.
All the silent, unspoken alarms.

The hair on the back of his neck grew stiff. The uneasiness stabbed at him, shapeless, having neither form nor meaning. Yet it was there, and the years had taught him not to ignore the messages that came on silent, unseen wings. He had spent a lifetime learning to read the signs that came from outside, the mark of a lead, the trail in the blade of grass, the turn of a bush, and the crumbled pattern of the soil. He knew the way of men and of all the creatures that walked, flew, or crawled. He understood the messages in their every step, their every flurry of wings, the alarms in their every cry and call.

He was the Trailsman, a part of the sounds and the ways of all nature and all the things of nature. He knew all he could see, smell, hear, taste, touch, but he also knew the power of those things that defied explanation, those messages that came from beyond the senses. Skye Fargo's lake blue eyes scoured the terrain as he ran one hand along the Ovaro's jet black neck. The horse had been the first to pick up trouble, as it so often did, and Fargo had absolute trust in the reliability of sensitivities beyond his own. The Ovaro's ears had been the first sign, suddenly moving back and forth, tilting forward, then flattening, then twitching to one side or the other. Then he felt the faint but unmistakable tension in the horse's black-and-white body and finally the short tattoo of hooves instead of the usual smooth stride.

Fargo let his eyes scan the land again, but there was nothing save the lush foliage of golden aspen and hackberry. The north Colorado territory was a rich land, ripe with foliage, flat with deep grasses, and mountainous with the northern conifers. Game abounded in this land—elk, bighorn sheep, cougar, fox, wolf, bear, and all the smaller creatures. But he saw nothing to give him alarm, yet the horse still beat a nervous tattoo with its hooves. Fargo steered the horse under the wide branches of a hackberry and swung to the ground. He let the horse calm itself in the shade of the big tree and continued to rub his hand soothingly against the warm fur. His eyes narrowing as they again traversed the terrain, Fargo heard the soft curse escape his lips and grew angry with himself.

Stupid. Ridiculous. He bit the words out silently as he swore at himself. Yet the moment had flung itself at him out of yesterdays, words he had scoffed at then suddenly whirling at him with a malicious fury all their own. They rose out of a moment three weeks back in the Oklahoma territory. He let a wry smile edge his lips. It had not been a completely bad experience. In fact, most of it had been damn nice, but it hadn't been the nice part that had suddenly leaped at him from out of the blue. He saw that the horse had calmed down, and he lowered himself to the ground and leaned back against the bumpy, gray bark of an old hackberry. He half closed his eyes and turned the days backward in his mind. Not that he had much choice, for they continued to stay with him, demanding to be relived again.

Part of it had been his own fault, the result of too much bourbon, too much money in his pocket, and too much of a warm, willing woman. It was a combination he had never been able to resist, and he saw no reason to do so then. The bourbon had been a reward to himself for a very long, very hot trail drive all the way up from Houston, filled with unexpected problems. The extra money was the kind of advance on a new job no reasonable man could turn down. The little town in the Oklahoma territory had a name, Stillwater, and he'd enjoyed the evening relaxing at the Stillwater Saloon as he looked forward to the room and bed he'd taken at the town inn. It was near midnight when he finished the last drink and walked the nearly deserted street toward the inn.

That's when he met her, standing beside the wagon, trying to close a tailgate that refused to close. He took in the wagon for a moment and saw it was an Owensboro Texas wagon outfitted with bows for a canvas top, big and bulky with the driver's seat under the canvas top. The wheels wore extra wide steel rims, he noted, one in the left rear bearing the ridged mark of a collision with a sharp rock. He turned back to the young woman to stare at lush, simmering beauty. Long, thick black hair fell almost to the middle of her back, dreaming deep brown, liquid eyes with thick, black brows that matched her hair. The liquid eyes, slightly almond-shaped, looked at him from out of an olive-skinned face with an aquiline nose and full lips that virtually quivered with sensuality. A scoop-necked, white peasant blouse revealed the deep cleavage of full breasts, and a black skirt covered womanly hips.

Fargo saw the liquid eyes slowly move across the chiseled planes of his face.

He took a step forward, curled one hand around the top edge of the recalcitrant gate, and, using his powerful shoulder muscles, pushed it closed. The hint of a smile touched the young woman's full lips. "Thank you. A handsome rescuer, a very handsome one. Thank you, again," she said. He immediately heard the accent in her speech, not one he could recognize.

"My pleasure. Don't usually get to help someone so damn beautiful," Fargo said.

Her smile was slow and simmering. "What do they call you, handsome man?" she asked, the faint accent intriguing.

"Fargo . . . Skye Fargo," he said. "And you?"

"Irina," she said.

"Never heard that name before. Where are you from?" Fargo asked.

"Hungary," she said, and Fargo nodded as he let his eyes go back to the Owensboro with its makeshift canvas top. Strange markings were painted onto the canvas, the outline of an eye, a triangle inside a circle, a crudely drawn hand holding a glowing candle between the third and fourth fingers, a cross standing upside down, and words he couldn't understand. "You have not seen our wagon before?" Irina asked.

"No," Fargo answered. "*Our* wagon?"

"It belongs to my brother and me," she said and had just finished the sentence when Fargo saw the figure trudging toward the wagon with a bucket of water. The man paused at the front of the wagon, a dark, brooding face on a stolid, slightly hunched body. "Mikhail," Irina said. The man grunted and stepped into the wagon with the bucket.

"He always so friendly?" Fargo commented.

"We have come a long way. It has been hard for him," she said.

"A long way from where?" Fargo asked.

"Hungary," Irina said. "We are Gypsies. Our family have been Gypsies for hundreds of years."

"How'd you wind up here?" Fargo frowned.

"A rich man paid me to tell his fortune, to read the cards for him every day, to give him the ancient wisdom of the Gypsies. He brought us here, and then he died. I told him he would," she said with a diffident shrug.

"And now?"

"I try to earn enough to go home someday. I tell fortunes. I read the cards," she said.

"The cards?"

"The tarot cards," she said.

"That all?" he questioned.

Her half-smile widened. "A girl must live, earn her way," she said and came closer, her deep breasts almost touching his chest, a faintly musky odor to her, strangely exciting. "For you, my handsome friend, I would give myself. You are too handsome to ask anything more. But Mikhail would be very angry, very angry," she said.

"Angry enough to beat you," Fargo asked.

"It's happened," Irina said. "He knows no other ways. Nobody will give him work here."

Fargo's hand slipped around the back of her neck. Her skin was warm and smooth under the thick, black hair, the musky odor of her again exciting. She was entirely too much woman to pass up. "I'm at the inn, room three," he said.

She nodded, and there was real heat in the liquid eyes. "I will tell your fortune, too," she said, and he pulled his hand away and walked on with a quick glance back at the Gypsy wagon. Irina had disappeared inside, and he hurried away. At the inn he undressed down to his undershorts and let a deep sigh of contentment escape as he stretched out on the luxury that was a bed. The Ovaro was in the stable, fed, groomed, and enjoying its own brand of comfort. They had both earned it, Fargo murmured silently.

The knock at the door was not long in coming, a soft yet firm sound. "It's open," he said, and she entered, halting at the side of the bed, liquid eyes taking in the smoothly muscled contours of his torso.

"The most handsome man I have seen in this big country," she said.

"I'm not going to disagree," Fargo said as Irina reached into her skirt pocket and brought out a small, stoppered bottle, two small clay cups each hardly larger than a shot glass, and a deck of cards.

"*Egri Bikaver*, wine from Hungary, for later, when I read the cards for you," she said, putting everything on top of the battered bureau against one wall. Her fingers, long and slender, were unbuttoning the white blouse as she returned to the bed. She pulled the blouse from her, and Fargo stared at the two full, deep, olive-skinned mounds, smooth and voluptuous, each tipped with a dark pink circle and in the center of each areola, a firm, red nipple. She undid the black skirt, it fell to the floor, and she stepped out of dark bloomers to stand before him, a throbbingly beautiful figure, deep breasts swaying slightly, round barrel chest beneath, and full, wide hips with a rounded belly that fit the rest of her lush body. A thick, inky triangle of unkempt hair stood out in perfect accompaniment to her, and just below, full-fleshed thighs that might someday be heavy, but were now only beautifully ripe.

His arms reached out, and she came down half atop him, the full lips on his, encompassing, working, sucking, and he felt her tongue reach out at once, wet caresses, harbinger thrustings, and the deep breasts were surprisingly firm pillows against his chest. His mouth found one, drew in the red nipple, and pulled on it. Irina uttered a deep, growling sigh, and felt her hands crawl down his body, across his groin and find his burgeoning organ. "Ah, good, yes, yes, aaaaaah . . ." she breathed as she stroked and pressed and drew her thighs upward. Her deep, thick triangle pressed against his groin, little soft-wire strands moving against his legs.

"Ah, good, is good, is good," Irina cried out as he let his hand find her wet warmth, and she almost threw herself onto her back, the full-fleshed thighs opening for him as he touched, and caressed, then reached into her silky tunnel. Irina's belly rose up, and slapped against his groin, growling gasps coming from her as she reached for him, closed her fingers around him, and pulled him to her. "Yes, yes, yes, please, good, oh, good," Irina cried out, and her musky odor was stronger, stimulating, an erotic perfume of the woman wanting without reserve. This was no performance, no charade of motion, but a body erupting in all its honest passion, and when he slid forward into her dark wetness, her breasts rose up, and she thrust forward, her hands pulling his head down to the olive-skinned mounds. Deep, growling gasps continued to come from her as she rose and fell with him, flesh urging flesh, passion feeding on passion, the spiral reaching upward, her fleshy thighs quivering around his hips as though they would never fall away.

Her cry remained a kind of growl even as it rose in pitch. "Ah, my God, aaaggggh . . . I come, I come for you, oh, handsome man, I come for you," Irina half screamed, and she came, and came again, and again, crying and bucking, smothering his head in the deep breasts until he wondered if she'd ever stop. But she did, finally, with a growling, guttural cry and sank down with him, clasped against him with all of her lush body. When her arms relaxed from around him and her thighs dropped from around his waist, she uttered another deep sigh. Finally, she pushed onto one elbow, then sat up, and the deep mounds swayed together as she met his stare, liquid eyes still swimming with their dark depths.

"Are all Gypsy girls like you?" he asked.

She gave a half-shrug. "Gypsies do not hold back. Passion is in our blood," she said. "Sometimes it is wasted. But with you it was all worth it."

"Take whatever you want from my jacket pocket," he said.

"Later. We do not need to talk of such now, not with you," Irina said, then swung herself from the bed. He watched her ample rear move as she walked to the bureau. She opened the little bottle and filled the two small cups, returned, and handed him one as she sat on the edge of the bed.

She raised her cup and drank it down in one gulp as he did his, the wine a full-bodied dark red, sweet yet not cloying. She took the emptied cups back to the bureau and returned with the deck of cards to sit cross-legged on the bed as she spread the cards on the sheet, and her lush nakedness seemed absolutely natural.

His eyes went to the cards she spread, then shuffled together, and he saw drawings on each, some that seemed witches, others naked women or fiery objects, and he noted four suits, one of swords, another wands, one of grails, and the last of pentacles. She mixed the cards again and put the deck in front of him. "Touch the cards. How you say, cut the deck," she said. He picked up the tarot cards, cut the deck, and handed them back to her. "That important?" he asked.

"Very. I read the cards for you. Now you have touched them, you have put yourself inside them. It makes it all stronger," she said and leaned forward as she shuffled through the cards, suddenly intensely studying the cards as she turned up one after another. Her full breasts hung forward, almost touching the cards, and he happily enjoyed the beauty of her. Suddenly, she stopped and sat up straight, and he saw the deep, liquid eyes turn even darker as she stared at him. "It is bad, very bad. The cards say it, they say you will be killed," she said, and he saw the furrow creasing her smooth brow.

Fargo allowed a half-smile. "They tell you when?" he asked casually.

"No, they do not say that," she answered.

"They tell you how?" he pressed, tolerance in his voice.

"Yes," she said, scanning the cards again and then looking back at him. "There will be a terrible battle. You will be torn apart, ripped to little pieces."

"Well, now, people have said I was going to be killed a lot of times, and they were always wrong." Fargo smiled.

"You do not believe the cards. That is bad. They never lie," Irina said, her voice growing agitated. She took the cards and pulled them together back into a deck, uncrossed her legs, and swept her skirt up, stepping into it quickly. The white blouse came next, and he saw the anger and concern in her face.

"Now, calm down," Fargo said evenly and started to reach out for her when suddenly Irina became two persons, separating in front of him. He halted and shook his head, and she swam back to one person. Fargo reached out again and felt the wave of dizziness sweep over him. He shook his head and saw Irina almost fade from his vision. "God-damn," he gasped, trying to move toward her, his legs suddenly made of lead. He felt himself falling forward to the end of the bed, and he shook away a gray curtain that had descended before his eyes. Irina came clear for a moment, watching him, and then the curtain descended again. His head fell forward to the foot of the bed. "Goddman," he heard himself muttering. "Goddamn." He felt the bedsheet against his face, but only for another moment, and then the world disappeared. "Bitch," Fargo murmured, but knew he was the only one who heard the word, and then there was nothing more.

FALCONER'S LAW
BY JASON MANNING

The year is 1837. The fur harvest that bred a generation of dauntless, daring mountain men is growing smaller. The only way for them to survive is the way westward, across the cruelest desert in the West, over the savage mountains, through hostile Indian territory, to a California of wealth, women, wine, and ruthless Mexican authorities.

Only one man can meet that brutal challenge—His name is Hugh Falconer—and his law is that of survival. . . .

from **SIGNET**

Prices slightly higher in Canada.   (0-451-18645-1—$5.50)